THE

OTHER

SIDE

OF

LIFE

D1518899

ANNA DRAZEK

THE OTHER SIDE OF LIFE

ANNA DRAZEK

ISBN 9798353818533

"Only the dead have seen

the end of the war. "

~George Santayana

THE OTHER SIDE OF LIFE

Table of Contents

THE OTHER SIDE OF LIFE

BOOK ONE

CHAPTER ONE

April 1939

A deep sense of melancholy overshadowed my father each time I asked about my mama. His eyes welled up and unhappy lines creased his face. Babula, my grandmother, wouldn't speak about her, either. The house quickly grew silent whenever I mentioned her name. One minute, laughter roared out from everyone's bellies. Then, the moment I mentioned her name or asked about her, the laughter evaporated, and the gloomy silence lingered for several minutes. In the silence, I could see the petrifying look on my Babula's face, my grandfather's gaze shifting from me to my father and back to me, and my father's fidgeting hands. Sometimes, my Babula pulled me away. Other times, my grandfather changed the subject. His point of reference was usually a joke that helped to lighten the upsetting mood. But I persisted and continued asking more questions about her until I turned six and my grandfather pulled me aside and told me about her. That was the first and last time anyone said anything about my mama.

In 1929, when my father met my mama, it was the best thing that could have ever happened to him. They met at a time when my father didn't believe that a pretty woman would ever fall in love with him. He wasn't the best-looking man in eastern Poland, but my mama didn't care about his looks. My father had a deep scar that ran from his left eyebrow, cutting across the dorsum of his nose and stopping a little under his right eye. With his looks, he could pass for a monster that scared off little children and women. But he wasn't born with the scar. His skin was smooth then, and his face was devoid of any blemish. He had gotten the scar in Kaluszyn in the summer of 1916. That was the year when two flour mills, a pot and pan factory, and a vinegar factory were established in Kaluszyn. It was the year when my grandfather's best friend opened a small bakery. It was the year when my father turned six. And it was also the year when my father's face was no longer the pretty one that had popped out of my Babula's belly.

My father spoke a lot about his childhood. He grew up in Kaluszyn with my grandparents. Many people who lived in

Kaluszyn were Jewish, and my grandparents belonged to this group of people. My grandfather was a shoemaker and my Babula was a tailor. My father enjoyed watching my Babula make dresses more than seeing my grandfather make shoes. That drove my grandfather crazy. His only son wasn't interested in his trade. My grandfather had frowned at it, and Babula had pleaded with him to ignore my father's interest, as he was still a child. Babula and my grandfather worked in a small workshop. Babula sewed dresses in one corner of the shop, while my grandfather made shoes in the other corner. The middle was my father's playground.

Small children liked to touch things. My father was driven by curiosity. It was a small workshop, but he succeeded in turning it into a playground. He touched anything he saw and climbed anything that looked like it could be climbed. His presence in the shop heightened Babula's fears. While she had no dangerous work tools laying around, my grandfather kept a vast array of tools in the shop, even tools that he didn't need for shoemaking. At times, curiosity took my father out of the shop. With his tiny hands and feet, he crawled out and into the street. Babula hurried after him and picked him up before he could get too far. Sometimes, he fell off the shelf that contained their work tools as he tried to climb up. Despite all his explorations, he usually came out unscathed.

Summer in Kaluszyn was usually very hot. My father played with the kids whose parents also had stores in the area. At six, he was skinny and shorter than most of the boys. This made it easier for other kids to bully him. He didn't fight or talk back to his bullies, which worried my grandfather.

"He can't even defend himself," my grandfather said.

My grandfather felt irritated each time my father returned to the shop or home crying, with torn clothes and bruised or bleeding skin.

"He is a man! He should fight back!" he would cry out.

"He is just six years old. Were you a man when you were six?" Babula would reply.

Olek was my father's biggest bully. He was nine years old and he always accompanied his father to his carpentry workshop. My father and his friend, Iwan, avoided Olek like the plague. However, on this day, Olek and his friends had surrounded them while they played football at an abandoned park some distance from the market stalls. My father arrived back at the shop with a nail stuck to his face and Iwan yelling, "He is hurt! Help! Help!"

That summer, my father determined that he would serve in the army to defend himself and the people he loved. But life had other plans for him. In 1929, he boarded a train to enlist in the army in Warsaw. He was the average height needed in the army, young, well-built, and agile. However, he was rejected after failing the military training. Serving in the army was his life-long dream. He had hoped that one day he would be a part of something great that would bring redemption to Poland. He went to Warsaw with so much hope that he would be recruited. Therefore, when he was rejected, he became depressed. Ashamed, my father didn't want to return to Kaluszyn after having spent three months in the military camp. However, ultimately, he decided to go back home and try again some other time. At the train station in Warsaw, he met and fell in love with my mama. There was something about my father that attracted my mama to him. They married four months later, and my mama moved to Kaluszyn to be with my father. I was born the following year.

In the early morning hours, my mama had tugged at my father's arm. He opened his eyes slowly and stared at the vague figure looking down at him.

"I think we are having a baby now," she said.

He said, half-awake, "What do you mean?"

"I think I might give birth now! Wake up, Filip!"

He jumped up from the bed and pulled her close to him. "Are you sure?"

"Yes. I am very sure."

He put his hands on her bare belly, then lowered his head and placed his ears on the belly.

"I'm having a baby! We're having a baby!" he said.

My father wrapped his arms around my mama, as she could no longer walk properly. Then she staggered backward and the two almost crashed to the floor. My father helped her sit on the bed.

"I'll be right back," he said.

"Where are you going?"

"To get help."

The nearest clinic was thirty minutes away, and my father couldn't risk it. Mrs. Petronela had a very good reputation when it came to delivering babies. Her house was a five-minute walk from our home. My father dashed out of the house barefoot and ran like a lunatic in the obscurity of the night. But when he returned with Mrs. Petronela ten minutes later, my mama and I lay on the floor, blood spattered everywhere.

———————

It was not unusual to have absolute silence in the house, but the unending stillness on this particular day made my skin tingle. Two nights ago, my grandpa and father had discussed some war that they thought would happen, though they weren't sure. Grandpa was sick, but that didn't stop him from ranting about the German and Polish governments. At eighty-five, he had vivid memories of all the fun and brutal events that had happened to him. Despite his terrific memory, his physical strength waned as time passed. The first time I realized that he would no longer be the grandpa I had always known was when I was seven years old. I had begged him to lift me and put me on his shoulders. He chuckled and stretched his two hands toward me. Gleefully, I allowed him to wrap his hands around me. He lifted me in the air, but his hands shook, and I could see raw fear in his eyes. Babula ran toward him and took me from his grip. He staggered backward and groaned. Then he settled on a chair, his hands still trembling. Babula told me that day that grandpa was getting sick.

He spent the rest of the day on the chair in the living room. He had a favorite sofa where he relaxed, and nobody was allowed to sit on it, not even me. Babula turned on the radio so that my grandpa could listen to it while he rested. Everyone agreed that the only thing my grandpa loved more than talking about the news was listening to it. He carried the radio with him everywhere he went in the house. It sat on a wooden stool next to the chair, and his eyes hovered around as he listened fastidiously. Sometimes he made remarks while the host presented the news. Other times he hollered and cursed.

I usually sat across from him, watching him listen. The host's voice went on and on about things I didn't understand, but my grandpa nodded his head as he listened. Grandpa said that I was more like him than my father was.

"He took after your Babula," he had said. "But you, my granddaughter, are much like me."

"How?" I said.

"You look like me, talk like me, and are intelligent and inquisitive like me."

But today, the silence in the house was nerve-racking. Babula was making dinner in the kitchen, and it was expected that I would be there to help out. But kitchen duty was something I hated.

"Babula?" I said.

She whirled around, her blonde hair tied in a bun. "Where've you been?"

"My room. How's Grandpa?"

"Not good. He can't use his legs anymore. His knees are failing."

"But he walked two days ago. He walked outside and wouldn't stop talking about the government."

She walked up to me and ran her hands through my hair. The smell of raw meat and onions lingered in the kitchen.

Her voice quivered. "Well, he couldn't get up this morning. We can only hope he gets better."

As Grandpa's health deteriorated over the years, Babula couldn't hide her fear any longer. She knew that she could lose him at any time. At eighty, she feared that she might die, too. Babula was a petite woman who had been beautiful when she was younger. She had met Grandpa when she was nineteen and he was twenty-four. It was love at first sight. Grandpa swore that he had never seen anyone as beautiful as Babula.

"It was her hair that caught my attention," he had said. "It was so long, I thought I had seen a mermaid. When she saw me, she looked away almost immediately, but I could catch the smile that appeared on her lips before she turned away."

"Give this to him," Babula said as she gave me a cup.

"What's this? Water?"

"No. It's medicine. It's good for him."

"Okay," I said. I took the cup from her and walked out of the kitchen.

Grandpa lay in his room. His condition had deteriorated over the years, and he could no longer walk. His mind was still somewhat astute, but not what it used to be. I stepped into his room, which smelled of urine and sweat. It was a medium-sized room with a queen-sized bed in the middle. Two pots of fresh green plants had been placed on both sides of the bed. He looked helpless, and I wished I could help him. I held the cup with both hands, afraid that I would spill the contents before reaching the bed.

"Grandpa," I called out. "Are you awake?"

"Yes."

"I brought you something to drink."

"What is it?"

"Babula said it's medicine."

"I'm tired of taking medicines."

"She said it's good for you."

"Tell her it's of no use. Medicines will not keep me alive much longer."

"I don't care," Babula said from the door. She took the cup from me and walked over to the bed. She placed the cup on the stool and caressed Grandpa's face. "You will not die on me."

"I'm eighty-five, Rosalia. Sooner or later, I will die. It's expected."

"I don't like the way you speak sometimes. Be happy! Optimistic! A miracle could happen."

"The only miracle I pray for is the avoidance of war. Unfortunately, I've seen it happen before, and I dread it."

Babula forced him to take medicine, then washed him with a damp cloth. Next, she rearranged the room and changed the sheets, replacing them with clean ones.

When my father joined my grandfather later in the evening, they spoke endlessly about the plausibility of a war. I hid behind the door and peeped through the crack, tilting my head now and then, hoping to catch a whisper of their conversation.

"There are speculations about the war. Sometimes I think it's best we leave, but we can't leave behind you and Mother," my father said.

"What are people saying? It's been difficult for me to listen to the radio these days. My chest thumps whenever it is on."

"Not much. Some say that Hitler is bluffing. Others say we shouldn't take anything lightly."

"What do you think?"

"I don't know what to think. Another war? It would be disastrous."

"We could win."

"Germany is-"

"I know it," Grandpa said. "I feel it in my veins that we will win."

"I have something to tell you."

"What is it?"

"I will be going to Warsaw."

"What for?"

"The army-"

"No," my grandfather said. He tried to sit up, but my father held him down.

"You are too weak to stand up."

"What are you thinking?" my grandfather snapped. He slapped my father's hands away.

"I should be in the army."

"What about Joanna?"

"She has you and Mama."

"That's nonsense, Filip. You should be here for her. What can Rosalia or I do for her? We are both old and-"

I backed away from the door, fear filling me. My father and grandfather spoke nothing good about past wars, and the thought of my father going away was terrifying. I whirled around and almost knocked over Babula.

"Joanna! Were you eavesdropping?"

My throat became sore and my lips quivered. Fear paralyzed me and I could no longer speak.

April 1939 was the year when things began to fall apart.

CHAPTER TWO

When we were children, Aleksander and I were inseparable. He was slightly taller than I was, and I was a year older than him. But that didn't stop us from acting like we were twins! We tried as much as possible to speak and act like twins. I pleaded with my father to purchase clothes that looked like Aleksander's, but my father always refused. Aleksander was the third child out of five. He had two older sisters and two younger brothers. I was the same age as Aleksander's immediate elder sister, and the eldest sister was a year older than me. However, I didn't get along with them, and they didn't get along with me. Aleksander's sisters, Hannah and Zofia, were snobbish and dressed ten years older than their ages.

Alexander's younger brothers, Jan and Lazor, were terrors. As little as they were, they made me tremble. Lazor was a seven-year-old midget with dark eyes that pierced one like a laser. He was a chatter-box, and his constant jabbering made my ears hurt. Jan was five years old and the opposite of his brother. He seldom said anything, and he always avoided eye contact whenever he spoke. However, he was a silent devil. He didn't have to move his lips to wreak havoc. He always threw sand at Aleksander and me. Sometimes Aleksander's brothers hid my shoes, and I had to look for them before returning home.

We used to spend a lot of time at his house, which was different from mine. Back at my home, the only chatter that could be heard was from my grandparents and father. Alexander's house was usually noisy. His parents fought a lot in the presence of their children and sometimes when I was there. Jan and Lazor usually ran around the house yelling and breaking things. At times, Aleksander and I joined them in running around and building sand houses. Hannah and Zofia were usually behind closed doors, discussing boys and dresses. Their conversations were fun to eavesdrop on. Sometimes Aleksander and I hid outside the window as we listened to them speak in hushed tones or squeal whenever one of them spilled a secret.

Everyone agreed that I had sharp ears. My ears were small, but they heard things from a thousand miles away. Those ears saved me from several punishments that I would have gotten from Babula. I always knew she was on her way to my room minutes before she opened the door. Sometimes, I heard the whispers of my father and grandfather floating in the air as they discussed crucial matters at nighttime. My sharp ears came in handy whenever we eavesdropped on Aleksander's sisters.

Aleksander's father, Yarognev, told us much about the University of Warsaw. Once a week, we sat down with him in the living room and he told us about Warsaw and the university. When I returned home and told my father and grandfather, they burst into uncontrollable laughter.

"Yarognev is just a fool," my grandfather said. "I bet you he hasn't visited Warsaw or attended the university."

"Why do you say that?"

"He is an uneducated man just like the rest of us. He thinks that talking to a bunch of kids about Warsaw will make him appear more intelligent than he is. I bet I can tell you more than what he knows. Your father, too. Remember, he was in Warsaw years before."

I didn't care about what my father or grandfather thought about Yarognev. He wasn't educated and had never visited Warsaw, but he knew so much about the place and was accurate with his facts. I knew he was accurate because when I asked my grandfather, he usually acknowledged the facts, but then dismissed them when I revealed that I had gotten them from Yarognev. Aleksander and I hoped that one day we would be able to attend the university.

"My father said that the university is so expensive that only the rich can afford it," I told Aleksander.

"That's what my father said, too. He wants me to be educated, but I guess that's not possible."

Yarognev and my father's hatred for each other was unexplainable. Each time I asked my grandfather why my father disliked Yarognev, he would say, "The man is just a fool! Ask your father."

And when I asked my father, he told me to ask my grandfather.

"Men and their egos!" Babula would say.

Their hatred for each other did not extend to me and Aleksander. I was allowed to go to Aleksander's house, but he wasn't allowed to come to mine. Whenever I asked my family if he could come over, my grandparents and father came up with several excuses.

"Don't you have other things to do?" my Babula said.

"Go and help your Babula in the kitchen. When you are done, you can go over to their house," my grandfather said.

"Just go to bed," my father said.

One day, my grandparents and father went to the synagogue without me. I had told them that I was ill. Babula was skeptical.

"I can take care of myself," I said.

"I know you can, but I don't feel comfortable leaving you behind."

"It's just an hour, Babula."

"Anything can happen in an hour. Now go and put on your kippah. We're running late."

"But Babula-"

"She's ill," my grandfather said. "She's going to be asleep the whole time."

"Yes! Asleep in our presence. We won't have to worry about anything if she's with us."

"I'm seven."

"And I am seventy-eight. What's your point?"

"I can take care of myself!"

Grandpa ruffled my hair. "Get some rest, kiddo!"

Babula's forehead creased as they left the house. I waited a few minutes, then dashed to Aleksander's house.

"Aleks! Aleks!" I cried out.

"What is it?" he said through the window. "What happened? Aren't you supposed to be at the Shul?"

"Aren't you supposed to be at the Shul, too?"

"I lied. I said I was sick!"

"I said I was sick, too!" I responded with a giggle.

He flew out of the house and we ran down the dirt road until we got to my father's home. Our bodies jerked to a standstill when we saw my Babula coming out of the house.

"You didn't even lock the doors!" she cried out. She had returned to instruct me to get some soup from the pot when I got hungry. Then, furious, she pulled our earlobes and we lumbered with her to the Shul. Babula had reported us to the rabbi, who sat us down after the sermon and told us the importance of obedience.

———————

Our favorite spot was a hill some distance from where we lived. If we climbed the trees there, we could see the roofs of a hundred houses. Aleksander and I played several games on the hill. We climbed the trees and ran up and down the hill to see who was faster. We also tried to guess whose house was whose by looking at the roofs. We had discovered the hill one evening while we were secretly following Zofia. Yarognev had complained that he didn't want her and Hannah going out anymore. Gossip had started floating around that Yarognev's daughters were uncultured and were always seen with men much older than they were.

"That's one of the reasons we don't want you going to that house," Babula had said. "Isn't Zofia the same age as you?"

"Yes. Why?"

"She's running faster than her age!"

Hannah and Zofia were on the lips of most of the women at Shul, and Babula didn't hesitate to indulge others about them.

One day, Aunt Maja visited Babula. She was Babula's closest friend, and their friendship had grown stronger when Aunt Maja's husband died. Her only child had died two years before her husband. Aunt Maja was tall. She was taller than my father, grandfather, and Babula.

"I wouldn't be surprised if one of them gets pregnant soon," Aunt Maja said, referring to Aleksander's sisters.

"I wouldn't be surprised, either."

"Isn't Joanna friends with them?"

"No," Babula said quickly. "She isn't friends with them. Rather, she's friends with the brother."

"Oh, yes! I see them around acting like twins! I still don't think she should be friends with that family."

"Well, she's just friends with Aleksander."

"But she goes over to their house to play with them."

"Just with Aleks."

I sat on the floor in the kitchen, listening to them talk about me as if I weren't there. Finally, Aunt Maja turned to me. "You talk to Zofia and Hanna?"

I shook my head immediately.

"You didn't say anything."

"No! I don't talk to them."

"Are you sure?" Babula said.

"I'm sure, Babula. I speak only to Aleksander and sometimes to his brothers."

"Jan and Lazor?" Aunt Maja said as if she didn't know who I was referring to.

I nodded. "Jan and Lazor."

"Not good," she said as she shook her head and waved her hands.

"But-"

Babula rolled her eyes, and I shut my mouth immediately. Aunt Maja adjusted her kippah as she helped Babula peel carrots. "Joanna should know how to cook some foods now," she said.

"Not yet," Babula said.

"Joanna? Is that true?"

"Um-"

"Come on, slice the carrots. I will watch you."

I stood up grudgingly and took the knife from her. She patted my back and chuckled.

"From slicing carrots to chopping vegetables. One day, you will be alone in the kitchen, stirring a pot of soup."

"Be careful, Joanna," Babula said.

"Oh, please! She can do this, right?"

I nodded. I held the knife with my right hand, listening as my heart pounded in my ears. So many things went through my head that day. First, I wished that Aunt Maja wasn't around. Whenever she was there, I found myself doing one chore or another. Second, I feared I would cut myself while slicing the carrots.

"Go on! The carrots will not cut themselves."

My face broke into a smile when I chopped the carrots successfully and poured them into a bowl. Aunt Maja touched my chin and smiled at Babula.

"You see, Rosalia? She didn't go blind. I don't know who keeps spoiling her more, you or Leon."

"It's Leon."

"I doubt that."

Aunt Maja picked up three slices of carrot and threw them into her mouth.

———————

I was unusually quiet that Saturday evening. I lay on the rocky ground with Aleksander, my eyes fixed on the sky. I hadn't slept the previous night. The thought of the war kept ringing in my head. Whenever I closed my eyes, I saw my father on the front line with other soldiers fighting for our freedom. Then a bomb exploded near him and his head became detached from his body.

Aleksander nudged me hard.

"What?" I snapped.

"You've been quiet. I've been talking nonstop and you haven't said a word."

"Oh."

"What's wrong with you? Did Babula offend you?"

"No."

"Are you pissed at your father?"

"No."

"Grandfather?"

"No."

"Then what is it?"

"My father wants to fight in the army."

"Why?"

"Why do people fight in the war?"

"But there is no war."

"My grandparents and father think that there will be war."

"My father hasn't said anything about the war, so I don't think there will be one."

"And what if there is war and the German soldiers come to Kaluszyn?"

He folded his right hand into a fist and raised it in the air. "We will fight!"

My body shook as I burst into loud, hysterical laughter.

"I'm serious!" he cried out.

"My grandparents say war is not good. They don't want to go through that again."

"My mother said she lost her parents during the war. But my father will not talk about it, even when Jan and Lazor beg him to. I guess something terrible happened that makes him act that way."

"Are you scared?"

"About what?"

"About the war, silly!"

"No. Are you?"

"A little. My grandfather has never said anything good about it, so I don't know how to feel."

"Tell your father not to go."

"He doesn't know that I know."

"How did you find out?"

"I overhead." A tear escaped from my eyes.

"Are you crying?"

I quickly wiped the tears from my face with the back of my hand. "I'm not crying."

"It looks like you are."

Clouds gathered above us and the sky became dark. Flashes of lightning appeared, followed by a loud crack of thunder. We jumped up and hurried down the hill to our houses. My dress was drenched by the time I got home. I hurried into the house and saw Babula in the living room, her eyes misted over with tears.

"Babula?" I said slowly as I approached her. My father grabbed my left arm and pulled me away from the living room.

"Where have you been?" he said.

"I was with Aleksander. We couldn't make it back in time before the rain started. Why is Babula crying? Is Grandfather fine?"

"Your grandfather is fine. He's sleeping."

I glanced at Babula, then whispered in his ear. "Then why is she crying?"

"Aunt Maja is dead."

I felt cold, not from the rain but from the bad news that had just come out of his mouth.

My voice quivered. "When did she die?"

"This morning. She died in her sleep."

"I don't-"

"Go to your room and change out of your wet dress before you fall sick! And don't bother Babula today."

I walked slowly to my room, shivering. I took off my clothes and dried my wet body with a towel. Then I sat on the floor of my room, naked. I wrapped my arms around my knees and fixed my eyes on the wall. Aunt Maja was dead, and that was all I could think about.

CHAPTER THREE

Two things kept me up that night: the thought of my father leaving me behind and Aunt Maja's death. Only two people close to me had died: my mother and Aunt Maja. I never knew my mama, so when I found out from my grandfather that she had passed away during childbirth, I was sad. I was sad because I wished I had known her, touched her, and listened to her speak. My only regret was not knowing her and that was the major reason for my sadness. But Aunt Maja's death struck something else in me. I had known her, touched her, and listened to her speak. I had heard of people dying, but I didn't know them. Aunt Maja's death was different. Her voice reverberated in my head. It was a deep voice that sounded as if a cat were stuck in her throat. She was a funny woman and I would miss her jokes.

Outside my room, I could hear Babula's faint sobs. I got out of bed and tip-toed toward the sound. She looked up at me when I entered the kitchen.

"Joanna?" she said, wiping away her tears. "What are you doing up so late? Go back to bed."

"I can't sleep," I said.

"You can't sleep? Why's that?" Babula asked.

"Aunt Maja," I said as I sat beside her. I sat in such a way that my knees were facing up, and my hands were wrapped around them.

"You should go to bed."

"I can't sleep."

"Aunt Maja is in a better place," she said.

"I know. You can't sleep because of Aunt Maja, too?" I asked.

"Yes," she said with a trembling voice.

"Is that how people die?" I asked.

"What do you mean?"

"I mean, do people just die in their sleep? Father told me she went to bed and didn't wake up."

"There are several ways people die, Joanna," Babula said.

"Mention a few."

"Oh, Joanna."

"It's okay. I'm not scared," I said, even though I was scared.

"You shouldn't be, but I would rather you go to bed now. You shouldn't be awake at this time."

"If I go back to bed, I won't stop thinking about Aunt Maja."

"I thought you said she was mean," Babula said.

I nodded. "She was mean. She made me do all those chores whenever she came over. But I liked her."

Babula chortled. "She was right, though. You should learn how to do those things."

"I know. Babula?"

"Yes?"

"Is my father going away?" I asked.

"Has he-"

"No. He hasn't told me anything, but I know. I know because I heard him tell Grandfather."

"It's just for a while. He will be back sooner than you think," she said.

"But I will miss him."

"I will miss him, too," Babula said as she tickled me. I burst into laughter and gently slapped her hands away.

Aunt Maja's sister arrived from Krakow two days after her sister's death. She was short and plump. She had begged Babula to help her sort through Aunt Maja's things, and Babula had begged me to accompany her.

We had visited Aunt Maja's house often. She was always delighted to see us. Aunt Maja had a problem concealing her emotions. Sometimes I wished she toned down her excitement.

Her house looked the same as it had when Babula and I visited Aunt Maja three days ago. While Babula and Alina walked toward Aunt Maja's room, I stopped in front of her daughter's room. Babula said Aunt Maja had refused to clear away her daughter's things when she died. She had left the room exactly the way it was. My fear spiked as I stared at the empty room. The bed was unmade and clothes were scattered across it. I placed my right foot into the room, then stopped. Cold air flushed through the window, and the wooden pane lashed against the wall. There was something bizarre about the room. It was almost as if Aunt Maja's daughter was there, staring back at me. Part of me wanted to leave, but curiosity tugged at me.

Babula said I was friends with Aunt Maja's daughter before I became friends with Aleksander. However, I had no memories of our friendship. That was expected, as her daughter had died at the age of four.

I entered the room. The smell of hibiscus lingered in the air. I whirled around and saw a pot of fresh hibiscus in the corner. A small wooden table sat in front of the window. I walked over to it. A miniature blue teddy bear lay upside down on the table.

"Joanna!"

I whirled around. My heart pounded in my ears. "Babula!"

"What are you doing?" she whispered as she beckoned to me with her hands.

I walked toward her. "Nothing!"

She grabbed my left hand and pulled me out of the room. "Aunt Maja's daughter died in there. If Aunt Maja were alive, she wouldn't want you invading her daughter's privacy. Stay away from there and don't touch anything unless I tell you to do otherwise."

I walked behind Babula as she led me into Aunt Maja's room. At first, I hesitated to enter.

"It's fine," Alina said. "Don't be scared."

I stepped into the room slowly. I was stunned to see Alina sitting on the same bed that Aunt Maja had died in. She didn't look scared. Babula also sat on the bed, and I was left standing.

"Have a seat, Joanna," Alina said.

"I'll stand," I said.

"We're going to be here for a while. Are you sure that's what you want?" she asked.

"Yes," I said.

I imagined Aunt Maja lying on the bed and laughing at me. It was something she would do.

"I don't know where to start. We have to sort out all of their things. I mean her stuff, Antoni, and Hannah," Alina said.

"That's a lot of things," Babula said.

"I know. Thank you for doing this with me. It wouldn't have been easy if I had to do all this on my own."

"It's not a big deal. What will you do with the house?" Babula asked.

"I don't want to keep it. It's weird, right? Three of them died in this house. It's unbelievable! This house is bad luck. I can't keep it. I didn't know I wouldn't see her again," Alina said as she wiped away tears with her handkerchief. Babula sat beside her in silence.

"You know I told her to come over to Krakow after Antoni's death, but my sister is so stubborn. She was so lonely. I wish I had spent more than with her. I wish I was around when it happened."

"She wasn't lonely," Babula said.

"How are you sure? She had no husband or child anymore. That was enough to cause her death," Alina said.

"I don't think loneliness was what killed her. Maja was one of the liveliest and most fun people I have ever met. She died in her sleep because it was her time to go," Babula said.

"I'm just a few months older than her. At some point, my time would come, too. Joanna?" Alina said.

"Yes, ma'am."

"What's in that drawer? Open it, let's see."

I opened a drawer and removed some of Aunt Maja's kippah, then laid them on a chair.

Alina burst into tears. "Oh! I remember asking her to give me that brown kippah, but she refused. She said it was her favorite." Alina drew the chair closer to herself. She picked the brown kippah and smelled it. "Do you want the rest of them?" she asked.

I exchanged glances with Babula.

"It's okay, you can have them. There are too many," she said as she counted eight kippahs. "You can take four and I will keep the rest."

I picked four kippahs and placed them on the edge of the bed.

"Do you like them?" Alina asked.

"Yes," I lied. I hated kippahs and I wished I didn't have to wear them each time we went to the Shul. They made my hair itch, and I had complained to Babula that they made me feel uncomfortable. But she had brushed it off.

My feet ached from standing for too long.

"Joanna," Alina said.

"Ma'am?" I answered.

"Come on, sit!"

I sat on the edge of the bed.

"There's enough space for the three of us. Maja is dead. She's not going to come back here to beat you for sitting on her bed," Alina said.

"You don't know that," I said.

She chuckled. "What do you mean?"

"You said it yourself. This house is bad luck!" I said.

"That…that was-"

"Don't pay attention to Joanna," Babula said.

"But it's true," I said. "Can I go outside?"

"Fine, go outside. Be careful," Babula said.

I stood up and hurried out of the house. As soon as I got outside, I breathed deeply. Then I released my brown hair from its high ponytail and allowed it to fall on my shoulders.

———————————

Our rabbi stood in front of everyone as he read Aunt Maja's eulogy. I sat between Babula and Alina, while my father sat behind us. Alina sobbed quietly as she sneezed into her handkerchief. Babula's eyes were swollen and I could tell that she was holding back tears. A cough echoed in the air and I looked up. When I turned around, my eyes hovered among the faces clouded with grief. I knew most of the people seated at the funeral service. They were frequent attendees of the Shul and some had been to our house. Madam Elenora sat in the front row with her husband. She wore a dark dress with a dark kippah, just like the rest of us. I had seen her occasionally talking to Aunt Maja, but I hadn't heard Aunt Maja say anything about her, so I wasn't sure if they were close friends.

I couldn't take my eyes off the casket that had been placed in front of us, between two large candles. I wondered if that was how my mama had been buried. I imagined her in a casket, placed in front of the people who loved and didn't love her.

After the sermon, Madam Elenora stood in front of everyone and began to sing. This time, Babula burst into tears. It was as if others were waiting for someone to break down the gate of tears, as they all followed suit. I didn't want to cry at the funeral service. I covered my face with my palms, hoping the tears wouldn't come. I was tired of crying, but there was nothing I could do. Tears flowed down my cheeks.

That night, my father came into my room.

"Are you asleep?" he asked, standing at the door.

"No."

He stepped inside and sat on the bed.

"How are you doing?" he asked.

"I'm fine."

"Are you sure?"

I nodded.

"With everything that has been going on, I wanted to make sure you are okay," he said.

"You should check on Babula. She needs this more than I do."

He waved his hands. "Babula is a grown woman."

"But Aunt Maja was her friend. Her only friend."

"True. But Babula is past that age where one worries about death," he said.

"What do you mean?" I asked.

"She's old and she has lost so many of her friends over the years. I don't think she's scared."

"But…but are you scared?"

"About death?" he asked.

"About Babula and Grandfather dying soon."

"I worry sometimes. But nobody lives here forever!"

"One day, we will all leave," I said.

"Yes. And never return."

There was a moment of silence before he told me about the army.

"I know. I heard when you were telling Grandfather," I said.

"You know I'm not leaving forever."

"Yes. Babula said you will be back after two or three months," I said.

"And I will get you some things from Warsaw."

"Yes! Alex's father said they have-"

"Forget what Yarognev said. He doesn't know what he is saying," he said.

A few days after the funeral, Alina left Kaluszyn and sold Aunt Maja's house. I kept Aunt Maja's kippahs in my room, hidden and out of sight. I couldn't bear the thought of wearing any of them. I imagined Aunt Maja appearing in my room and giving me a knock for putting them on.

Babula seemed to have moved on after the funeral. She no longer cried.

I told Aleksander about Alina, Aunt Maja's kippahs, and the funeral.

"Why didn't you come to the funeral?" I asked him.

"My father said no."

"No? Why?" I asked.

"He didn't want anyone to go. He hated Aunt Maja. Nobody in my family likes her. My sisters despise her," he said.

I understood that. Aunt Maja didn't hide her dislike for their family. She complained to Babula that she didn't like the way I was always around Aleksander.

"What if Joanna is using Aleksander and deceiving us?" she had asked Babula one day.

"What do you mean?" Babula responded.

"Look at it this way," she had said. "What if she is friends with Hannah and Zofia, and she's hiding under the pretense that she's friends with Aleksander?"

"She's too young to do something like that," Babula said.

"Hannah and Zofia are young girls and yet see what they do."

"I trust Joanna."

"Do you trust Aleksander and his clan?" Aunt Maja asked.

Babula shook her head. "No, I don't."

Aunt Maja hadn't done a good job of hiding her dislike for them.

"Did they ever do anything to you?" Babula asked.

"No. But sometimes there are some people whom, no matter what happens, you just don't like. That family is a typical example of what I am talking about."

Aleksander burst into laughter when I told him that I hid the kippahs.

"My father said dead people don't come back," he said. "Aunt Maja is gone and she will not get mad at you for wearing any of her things. Her sister gave them to you, right? So it's not like you stole from her."

"What if dead people come back?" I asked.

"Then my father's mother would have been back a long time ago, with the way my mother always throws curses at her. She would be turning in her grave," he said.

"I felt it."

"You felt what?" Aleksander said.

"The dead."

"Don't be ridiculous!"

"I'm serious!" I said.

"How? When? Tell me!"

"In Aunt Maja's house."

"That's a lie!"

"I'm not lying!" I snapped.

"Fine. Explain," he said.

"In Aunt Maja's daughter's room. I felt her presence."

He rolled his eyes.

"I swear! It felt like her daughter was in there. And then in Aunt Maja's room and eventually the whole house. It was creepy. Three people died in that house the exact same way. Asleep!"

"That's spooky!" he gasped.

————————

Two weeks before my father left, he brought home a fluffy brown Pomeranian puppy.

"Where did you get him?" I asked, excited.

"Does it matter? What will you call him?" he asked.

"Um…I don't know…Jasper?"

He chuckled. "Jasper? Why Jasper?"

I shrugged my shoulders. "Because he looks like a Jasper. And Aleksander swore that his grandma named him Jasper, but his parents hated the name. But I like it!"

I took Jasper along with me when I went to visit Aleksander. However, Aleksander wouldn't come near Jasper.

"C'mon! He doesn't bite!"

"I don't like dogs," he said.

"Why not?!" I asked.

"I don't know! I just don't like them."

Jan and Lazor loved playing with Jasper, unlike Aleksander, who wouldn't let the dog come close to him. His sisters couldn't care less about Joanna or the dog.

"Why did you name her Jasper?" Jan asked.

"Him. Jasper is a male dog."

"Okay. So, why did you name him Jasper?"

"I like the name," I said.

Jan pulled his tail and I slapped his hand. "Stop it!" I said. "That hurts him."

"How do you know that?" he asked.

"I just know."

He pulled his tail again and I slapped his hand.

"What's your problem?" I said.

"Did Jasper tell you that he is in pain?" he asked.

"How would you feel if someone pulled your legs and dragged you on the floor?" I asked.

He chuckled. "It would be fun!"

He pinched Jasper's nose and Jasper bit him.

"Ouch!" he cried out.

"That's what you get for being mean," I said as I stuck out my tongue. Tears poured from his eyes. He stood up and ran back into the house.

When I was about to go back home, I couldn't find Jasper.

"Maybe he has gone back home," Aleksander suggested.

"No, he did not! Jasper would never do that! Help me find him! Jasper! Jasper!"

"Jasper! Jasper!" Lazor yelled.

My eyes welled up with tears and I fought hard to resist the urge to cry. My father had gotten Jasper for me with the hope that Jasper would keep me company while he was away.

"If I don't find Jasper, I will pluck out your eyes!" I cried out.

"But I don't know where he is!" Aleksander said.

Finally, I found Jan at the back of the house with a shovel in his hands, burying Jasper.

"What are you doing?" I yelled. "What are you doing to Jasper?"

"Go away! Go away!" Jan yelled.

I ran toward them. Someone jumped in front of me with a shovel in his hands. I saw wickedness burn in Lazor's eyes.

"I won't let you go there!" Lazor said.

I lurched at him and he waved the shovel at me.

"Get away!" I said.

"If you move closer, I will hit you with the shovel," he said.

I whirled around, disoriented. "Aleks! Aleks! Aleks!"

"He's not here, and even if he was, he wouldn't be able to save you."

"Aleks hates dogs!" Jan said. He was putting Jasper into the hole he had dug. Jasper whined as Jan covered him with sand.

"Aleks!" I called out again. "This isn't funny, Jan! Stop it! Stop it!"

"He bit my hand!" Jan cried out. "Your stupid dog bit my hand!"

"Joanna!" Aleksander yelled.

I whirled around. "Aleks! Hurry, help! Jan and Lazor are burying Jasper."

"What?" he said as he ran toward us. He jumped at Lazor and the two struggled on the ground. Adrenaline rushed through my veins. I ran toward Jan and pushed him to the ground. Quickly, I started digging Jasper out of the ground. Jan held my left hand and tried to pull me away. I picked up a handful of sand and threw it into his eyes. He let out a loud cry.

Yarognev came rushing into the backyard. "What's happening?"

I dug Jasper out quickly. Too distraught to utter a word, I hugged Jasper tightly and walked away. That was the last time I visited their house.

CHAPTER FOUR

I was still mad at Aleksander. For three days, I had barely seen him and I tried to avoid him at all costs. I went to the hill at times when I knew he wasn't going to be there. I sat with Babula and my father during services. Most times, we sat together in Shul except when Aunt Maja insisted that I sit with her and Babula. That day, I sat with Babula and my father, while Aleksander sat with his siblings and parents at the back. He tapped my shoulder, but I ignored him. I didn't want to look at his face. It wasn't his fault and it was wrong for me to hold him accountable for what his brothers had done to Jasper, but I was consumed with rage. He tapped me again and I ignored him. I fixed my gaze on our rabbi and pretended to be listening to him, but my mind was far away.

Just like every other day, I never listened to our rabbi. Sometimes, Babula asked me questions immediately after we got back home.

"What did he talk about today?" she asked.

I swallowed the spit in my throat. Even when I listened to our rabbi, I forgot everything he said the minute we got back.

"I'm talking to you, Joanna. What did the rabbi say?" Babula asked.

"She's just a child, Rosalia, leave her alone," Grandfather said.

"How is she going to grow up to be a good daughter if she doesn't know what being a Jew is all about?" Babula asked.

"She'll learn with time," my father said.

I knew what being a Jew meant. I just didn't remember what our rabbi taught in Shul. Babula pulled my ear and I cried out in pain.

"What did he say?" she asked again.

"I can't remember!" I said.

"That's because you don't listen!" she said. "How will you learn when you don't listen?"

"My ear! My ear!"

I tried hard to pay attention to the rabbi, but it was difficult. My mind was always preoccupied with random thoughts. Sometimes I thought about a dragon chasing Aleksander and me. Other times, it was a tree chasing us. One time, I daydreamed about being abroad. I was in London, having fun with the Englishmen. However, on this day, I was boiling with anger. If Aleksander had touched me one more time, I would have turned around and slapped his face.

After the service, Aleksander ran to me while I walked back home with my father and Babula.

"Joanna! Joanna!" he called out.

"Are the two of you fighting?" my father asked.

"Yes," I said.

"What happened?" he asked.

"Jan tried to bury Jasper."

"I told you to stay away from them, but you wouldn't listen. You never listen!" Babula said.

"Why would Jan do that to Jasper?" my father said.

"Because he is evil. Jan and Lazor are demons!"

"You don't call a human being that," Babula said, "But since it's them, I guess you can."

My father touched my chin. "Forgive your friend. It's not good to hold grudges against the people we love."

"But they hurt Jasper!" I cried out.

"They? Was he involved?" my father asked.

I shook my head. "No."

"Then you should be mad at Jan and Lazor, not him."

I whirled around and rolled my eyes at Aleksander.

"Come home quickly," my father said.

"Come home quickly? No, she's going home with us," Babula snapped. "Make peace with your fake twin quickly. We don't have all day to wait for you!"

"I'll hurry," I said as I walked toward Aleksander.

"You won't talk to me," Aleksander said. "Why?"

"You know why."

"But…but it wasn't me who wanted to bury Jasper. You know I don't like dogs," he said.

"It wasn't you, but it was Jan and Lazor. So it was you, too!"

"I helped you free Jasper, remember?"

I rolled my eyes again. He was right. If he hadn't helped me, Jasper would have been dead. However, I didn't want to admit it. I folded my arms across my chest. "I don't care!"

"I'm sorry! It won't happen again," he said.

I pouted my lips.

"Forgive him already!" Babula cried out.

"Fine, I forgive you. I meant what I said earlier. If you or any one of your brothers comes close to Jasper, I will pluck out all of your eyes and feed them to Jasper."

"Fine!" Aleksander said.

We hugged each other and I hurried to join Babula and my father. My father put his hand around my shoulder as we walked back home. Attending Shul was different without my grandfather and his never-ending jokes. He no longer followed us to the Shul because of his sickness. This made him grumpy all of the time.

"I'm tired of lying on the bed all day!" he complained.

"It's not like you have a choice. You need to rest," My father said.

"Rest? That's basically all I have been doing. Rest, rest, rest! I'm beginning to go crazy."

When I wasn't outside playing, I was with my grandfather in his room, massaging his feet and telling him about my day. I told him about Jan and Lazor and how they had wanted to bury Jasper.

"That's evil!" he said. "Don't ever go back there again. Those kids are too little to do something like that. I'll tell your father to speak to Yarognev. That man and his wife need to do something about those terrible kids they are raising."

"Aleksander is different," I said.

"How so?" he asked.

"I don't know, but he is just different. He is not mean like his brothers, and he does not snub me like his sisters."

"I hope he continues to remain different. If not, it's best that you stay away from him."

"I will. I was told to say hi to you," I said.

"By who?"

"Many people, including the rabbi and Mr. Borys."

Grandfather chuckled. "Oh, Borys my good friend. I haven't seen him in a while."

"Yes, he said he would check up, but first he has to travel."

"Where is he going?" he asked.

"He didn't say, but he said he will tell you all about it when he comes back."

My father entered the room.

"Joanna," he said. "I need to talk to your grandfather alone."

"Okay," I said.

I stood up and walked out of the room. My father shut the door. Jasper ran toward me and licked my feet. Then, he ran toward Babula, almost making her trip. Just like Aleksander, Babula had a problem with Jasper.

"I don't know why we have to leave this dog in the house," Babula said.

"His name is Jasper," I said.

"I know his name."

"Then call him his name."

She placed her hands on her hips. "Jasper. His name is Jasper. Now get him out of my sight before I fall and break my hip."

I carried Jasper and kissed him on his face.

――――――――――

I cried the day my father left Kaluszyn. The night before, I couldn't sleep. I kept tossing and turning. I had never been apart from my father, and I didn't know what it felt like to be away from him. I knew some kids who hardly saw their fathers. Their fathers worked in other towns and came home a few times a month. They envied me and always asked what it felt like to have my father around. Now I would be one of those kids whose fathers weren't around.

My father had packed his bags the previous morning and was now having a conversation with my grandfather. I waited in the living room with Babula.

"I will write him every day," I said.

"He has not left yet and you are already sad."

"Aren't you sad?"

"Your father is a grown man. I will miss him, but I am not sad. It's just that there will be no one to help me take care of your grandfather when your father leaves."

"I'm around. I can help you with that."

"I know, but you don't have the strength that your father has. Can you lift your grandfather and help him use the toilet?"

"No," I said.

"I don't have the strength to do that, either, but I will manage."

"We will do it together."

She ran her hands through my hair and smiled. "Of course we will do it together."

I heard my name from outside. "Joanna!"

"Is that Aleksander?" Babula said.

"Yes."

"What is he doing here?"

"I told him to come," I said as I dashed out of the house. "Aleks!"

"I was so worried. I thought you all had left already."

"We are about to go to the railway station. My father is still talking with my grandfather."

"Great! Will he bring stuff for you from Warsaw?"

"He should. I told him not to bring a lot of things when he comes back. I hope he remembers."

Aleksander and I chatted on our way to the train station. My father and Babula walked behind us. We held each other's hands and cracked jokes. Each time I turned back, I noticed the sorrow on Babula's face. She was sad, but she wouldn't admit it.

We passed an elementary school. We usually walked by it whenever we came back from the hill. Each time we did, I begged Aleksander to stop at the school and watch what they were doing.

At the railway station, Babula began to cry. My father consoled her.

"It won't be long before I get back," he said.

"Be careful."

We hugged each other before he boarded the train. We didn't leave the railway station until the train was out of sight. On our way back home, none of us said a word.

———————

I spent the rest of the day in my grandfather's room. Jasper walked about. The house was silent and it was obvious that we all missed my father already. After a while, my grandfather fell asleep, snoring loudly. My grandfather's snores were usually very loud, although he always argued that he didn't snore at all.

"You do snore!" Babula would snap.

"I don't!"

"Yes, you do."

"Joanna!"

"Yes, Grandpa."

"Do I snore?"

I would chuckle. "Of course, Grandpa. Your snores wake me up at night."

My father and Babula would burst into laughter.

I lay on the floor and Jasper ran to me. He licked my face and played with my hair. I wished my father had taken me with him to Warsaw. I wished he hadn't left me behind. I tried to picture what it was like on the train with my father. I would have sat at the window because I would have wanted to watch what was going on outside as we moved.

My father promised to write us immediately after he got to Warsaw. I could not wait to read his letters. I promised to write him too, and he said he would try as much as possible to reply to my letters.

"I might not be able to reply to your letters on time," he said.

"Why not?"

"I don't know how strict the rules are this time around, but I promise that I will try to write and reply to your letters as soon as I can."

I shut my eyes and tried to imagine what it would be like when he returned.

"Day one," I said as I counted with my fingers. This was the first day of the many months he would be away from home. I didn't have to worry because he would be back soon.

CHAPTER FIVE

May 1939

Fear gave way to panic when we didn't receive a letter from my father a few weeks after he left for Warsaw. Babula couldn't sleep and she threw questions at my grandfather.

"I don't know," my grandfather always replied.

"But he should have written to us. It's been weeks!"

"Maybe he hasn't gotten a way to write to us yet," he said.

Babula sent me to the post office to check on whether a letter had arrived for us. I usually ran to the post office with Aleksander. We turned it into a game. Aleksander was a faster runner, and he always got there before I did. Each time, we got the same answer.

"No letter yet!"

However, on the 28th of May, we received a letter from my father, four weeks after he left for Warsaw.

"Read it again," my grandfather said with excitement.

I held the letter close to my face and read it out loud. Babula and grandfather listened attentively. Sometimes my grandfather told me to repeat a sentence. Other times, I repeated a paragraph.

Warsaw,
May 28, 1939

My Dearest Joanna,

How is everyone back at home? How are you? How are Babula and your grandfather? Is your grandfather's health improving?

Where do I start? I had everything planned out in my head. Forgive me if this letter sounds like I am raving like a madman. I am sorry that I have not been able to write as much as I want to. The rules are pretty strict here, and I just now found a way to write back! I hope you get this letter. If you do, write me back and tell me everything that has been happening in Kaluszyn. I will reply through this channel. You don't want to know what I did to write this letter!

As you can see, I arrived in Warsaw safely. But I had to go to camp immediately. Things are really great here. Tell your grandfather that we are preparing for a war we hope will not happen. Most of the recruits are mean, just like Jan and Lazor. However, I have made a very good friend here. His name is Garwel Nowak. He is a nice person and he has a daughter around your age. I've told him a lot about you, and he would love to meet you someday.

I miss Babula's cooking! Here, we eat weird things. I don't know if I can call what we eat good food. I guess it's part of the training.

Joanna, remember my bushy hair, which your Babula always complained about? Guess what? It was shaved immediately after I arrived at the camp. I'm bald now. You would laugh if you saw me. Your baba will be an army officer soon! I can't wait to show you and everyone else that your father is now an army officer.

You won't believe this, but I miss your friend, Aleksander. It's funny, right? Say hello to him!

Oh, I almost forgot Jasper! Keep him safe and away from Jan and Lazor.

Say hello to Babula and your grandfather.
I miss you!

With Love,
Your baba,
Filip.

The letter came at a point when we were about to give up! Immediately after reading the letter, I sat on the floor and began writing my reply. Babula sat beside me, her eyes hovering around the letter as she gave me instructions on what to write.

Kaluszyn,

May 29, 1939

Dear Baba,

I hope this letter finds you well. Babula is sitting with me as I write, and we are in the room with Grandfather. We were worried when we did not hear from you. Babula and Grandfather sent me to the post office every day to check on whether your letter got lost there. Aleks always went with me, and we turned it into a game. A racing game! Aleks always wins, but I hope to beat him one day.

We are glad that you are well. We are also well, baba. I miss you! Everyone here misses you! Nothing much has been happening and Kaluszyn is just as you left it. Home is boring, but thanks to Aleks and Jasper, I'm a bit entertained. Oh, and I won't forget to tell Aleks that you asked after him! Jasper misses you, too!

Grandfather said I should tell you that you shouldn't worry about us. In your next letter, he wants you to tell him more about the supposed war and the rumors flying around in the camp. Will there be war? Should we be worried?

Baba, you didn't mention Garwel Nowak's daughter's name. I would like to know it. What's she like? Is she funny like me? Does she like dogs? I've never had a female friend and I wonder what it would be like to have a friend other than Aleks. Aleks will be angry when he hears that I want a friend other than him.

Babula and I are the only ones who walk back from the Shul after service. It's boring without you and Grandfather. I can't wait for you to come home.

With love,
Grandfather, Babula, and Joanna.

June 1939

For the first time in my life, my father wasn't around for Shavuot, which was one of the Jewish holidays he loved. My grandfather couldn't participate the way he wanted to. I enjoyed every part of Shavuot except the fact that we had to read the book of Torah. I made sure to fake a smile during Torah because I didn't want to upset Babula. Aleksander hated the holiday. He hated everything involving Shavuot, from the plants used to decorate to the fact that we had to spend all night reading the book of Torah.

Babula and I spent the previous weeks looking for the perfect plant to decorate our home.

"I want something different this time," she said.

Babula made sure she showed my grandfather each flower we got.

"What do you think about this?" she asked him.

He waved his hands at her. "They are fine."

"That was what you said about the rest of the flowers. I keep telling you that's not how it works. You have to select the best."

"Oh, Rosalia, you do things like this all the time!"

"What do I do?" she cried out.

"You make me choose from a bundle of flowers every year and you end up selecting what you want. You don't even listen to my opinion."

"That's because I don't trust your opinion."

"Then why do you keep asking? Just let Joanna choose the flowers for you."

"She's a child! She doesn't know what she's supposed to select!" Babula snapped.

I watched Babula as she arranged the plants and flowers accordingly. Each year, she was enthusiastic about Shavuot.

"We are not going to have our house decorated in time if you continue to stand there!" she said to me.

"I'm sorry, Babula," I responded as I hurried to help her place the flowers around the house.

Last year, I had fallen in love with the decorations at Aleksander's house. I was tempted to see what they had done this year. However, after what his brothers had done to Jasper, I had made up my mind to never set foot in their house.

Aleksander had come over to our house. Though Babula didn't want him around, she made an exception because she needed his help. Babula had asked him to assist us with the decorations.

"I hate Shavuot," he said.

I placed a finger on my lips. "Shhh!"

"What?"

"Don't let Babula hear you."

"Why? What will she do to me?"

"She doesn't like you already. Things like that will make her prevent you and me from being friends!"

"Then I will just have to pretend that I like Shavuot!"

After about four hours of putting plants and flowers over the house, Babula wasn't pleased with the results. She wanted to start all over again. I ran to my grandfather.

"She's going to make us start all over again! Do something!"

"We?"

"Yes! Aleksander and me! He's helping out."

"What is wrong with the decorations this time around?"

"She said it's not good enough!" I cried.

Every year, the decorations weren't good enough for Babula. She was always close to tearing them down. My father and grandfather always talked her out of doing that.

Aleksander and I waited outside as Grandfather spoke to Babula.

"What do you think will happen?" Aleksander asked.

I shook my head. "I don't think she will do it."

"Why?"

"Grandfather will talk her out of it. He always talks her out of it. Besides, I doubt that she has the strength to redo everything."

But when she came out of the room, she began taking down some of the decorations.

"I thought you said she wouldn't do that?" Aleksander said.

"I didn't think she would!"

We redid the decorations. She liked them a bit better than the first set, but she would have taken them down again if not for the sharp pain in her back.

My father and grandfather were usually the ones who made the royzelech, or little roses with paper cut-outs, that we used to decorate our windows. Grandfather couldn't do it for us because his hands weren't steady enough to cut the paper.

"Can you make the royzelech?" Babula asked Aleksander.

He glanced at me, then at Babula. I knew he could do it, but he hated Shavuot. Plus, he had complained when he helped us with the decorations.

"Can you make it?" she repeated.

He shook his head slowly. "No, I can't do it."

I gasped!

Babula faced me. "What is it?"

Aleksander looked at me as he batted his eyelashes.

"Nothing."

"Nothing?" she said, her arms folded across her chest. "Are you going to lie to me?"

"No, Babula."

"Who makes the royzelech in your house?" she asked him.

"My father."

"And you never helped him make them?"

"Sometimes."

"That means you can make them?"

"No."

"But you have an idea?"

He shook his head.

"I remember now," Babula was saying, "Last year, Joanna came home with one in her hand and she said you made it for her. She didn't stop talking about how you had made it by yourself, and she placed it on her window. Until one night we couldn't find it anymore. My point is that you know how to make those paper cut-outs and you are lying."

He nodded slowly. Babula hurried to the room to get the materials needed to make the paper cut-outs. Aleksander showed us how to do them. Later that day, we sat at the table, making the paper cut-outs. After a few minutes, Aleksander said he had to go home.

"Thank you!" Babula said. "You were of great help to us. Say hello to your parents and tell them that I would love to pay them a visit. After Shavuot, of course!"

Babula was lying. She would never visit them even if a gun were pointed at her head. And she wouldn't have been comfortable having Aleksander inside the house if she hadn't needed his help for Shavout.

We cut the rest of the papers in silence. Last year and the years before, it was my grandfather and my father who had sat at the table making the cut-outs. They usually did the cutting as they discussed several topics. Politics and religion were their favorites.

"The stress we have to go through to make all these," Grandfather said. "Are all these necessary?"

"If you ask all these questions," Babula said as she put a plant at the center of the table, "what do you expect little Joanna to say? Please don't be a bad example to her."

"Bad example? We are here making the paper cut-outs. How is that a bad example?"

"We are setting a good example, Mama," my father said.

"Well, set a good example without complaining about being Jewish!"

"I love being Jewish," my father said. "But I don't know about a certain person sitting at the table and making paper cut-outs!"

I chuckled. "He is talking about Grandfather!"

"Of course, he is talking about me! Don't listen to your Babula and father. I love being Jewish! It's my pride," Grandfather said.

Other times, they spoke about the government and how they felt things were getting better or worse for us. They had spoken about relocating abroad.

"London will be a good start for you and Joanna," Grandfather said.

"What about you and Mama?" my father asked.

"This is our home."

"This is our home, too. If we are going to leave, we would leave with you and Mama. You like London?"

"Why did you ask that?"

"You always suggest we go there."

"I had friends who left with their families during the wars. They were going to London, but I don't know if they made it. That was many years ago."

"Why didn't you leave?"

"My father didn't want to leave."

"Just like you don't want to leave?"

"Your mama and I are old. We don't have the energy to move around."

We spent the night at the Shul, learning the Torah. Babula said it was important that we spend the night learning the Torah because we were making up for the mistakes our ancestors had made. The Jews had slept the day the Torah was to be given. Now we were deprived of our sleep because of what they had done. I always wondered why we had to be punished for what they did, but Babula said it was a privilege and not a punishment. However, it was a punishment for me.

Before we read the Torah, we stood for hours, meditating and reciting the Amidah, which was the standing prayer. I looked to the right and saw Aleksander with his family. He beckoned to me to come over and sit with them. He was sitting with his brothers while his parents sat in front of them. His sisters sat behind them and looked like I did, lost. I glanced up at Babula. Her eyes were shut, as she was invested in the prayer. I looked around. Nobody seemed to be paying attention to me or Aleksander. I threaded my way through the people seated on the same bench as us, quietly saying, "I'm sorry," as I stepped on some people.

Aleksander rolled his eyes. "My legs are shaking!"

"Me too. And I am bored."

He grabbed my hand. I followed him out of the Shul and we hid on a farm behind it.

"I tell you, the only thing I look forward to is the feast. Nothing more!" he said.

"You complain a lot, Aleks."

"I'm not complaining! I'm just bored. Everything about Shavuot is boring! Why do we have to spend the rest of our day here when we could be having fun-"

"Or sleeping." I didn't feel comfortable staying outside and hiding between crops. "Let's go back inside."

"I thought you said you hate it in there."

"More than you can imagine, but if Babula doesn't see me standing beside her when she opens her eyes, she's going to go crazy. I don't want her to go crazy."

"It will be fun!"

"Fun for you!"

I knew his parents didn't care less if he was around. Babula didn't approve of the way his parents trained their children. That was one of the reasons why she didn't want me around them. She didn't want me to get spoiled.

"Who allows their kids to act like that without spanking them?" Babula had asked when Jan and Lazor pushed a boy into the gutter, causing him to bleed heavily. "That woman didn't say anything! Nothing! If Joanna ever does something like that, I'm not going to turn a blind eye."

Or she complained about the children when they didn't attend Shul with their parents.

"Did you notice that the girls weren't at the Shul with their parents today? I wonder what they are doing at home instead of being here."

"Maybe they are sick," my father said.

"Sick? Both of them? That can't be true."

"Maybe you should go over there and ask them why their daughters aren't here today," my grandfather said.

Babula rolled her eyes. "I would have asked them, but unfortunately we are not friends with them."

"All the more reason why we should mind our business."

A man turned back and peered at us. "Shh," he said.

"Now you are preventing some people from listening to the rabbi," Grandfather said.

Babula nudged him.

My body itched as the grass touched my skin. "Let's go inside."

"A few more minutes."

"That's what you said the other time."

"Let's play a game."

"Now?"

"Yes."

I whirled around to see if anyone was coming.

"What kind of game?"

"Let's play-"

We heard footsteps approaching. Quickly, we crouched and hid behind a tree. Then we heard whispers flying.

"I saw them going that way," a voice said.

We looked at each other, fear in our eyes. Then a hand grabbed me. It was Babula.

CHAPTER SIX

August 1939

In June, a family moved into our neighborhood in Kaluszyn from Warsaw. The husband, Mr. Vasilli, was a new teacher at the elementary school in Kaluszyn. They had two boys who were much older than Aleksander and me. One day, after service in the Shul, Mr. Vasilli told Babula that he wanted to give me some books that his sons had owned when they were my age. That was when I got introduced to Jan Brzechwa, my favorite poet. At that moment, I knew I was going to be a writer.

I spent most of my time reading the books he gave me. When I didn't understand what the writer meant, Mr. Vasilli was always willing to explain it to me. Reading the books kept my mind off my father. We had not heard from him since he had sent the letter in May, and my grandparents were worried. One day, I overheard them discussing my father.

"What if something bad has happened to him?" Babula asked.

"He is fine," my grandfather said.

"You don't know that."

"He said the rules there are strict. Perhaps it has been difficult for him to reply to our letter. Or maybe he hasn't received the letter we sent to him."

"It is almost three months. How long should it take? I just want the letter as reassurance that he is fine," Babula said.

"You shouldn't be too worried. Filip is a grown man. He can take care of himself," my grandfather said.

"Haven't you heard the news? There could be war, and some people are already planning their exit. I'm more worried about Joanna. She's just nine years old and she cannot take care of herself alone. What if something happened to Filip? She has already lost a mother. It would be tragic if she lost him, too."

"But she has us," he said.

"You can barely walk without my assistance and I'm just surviving. I'm breaking down as each day passes," she said.

"Don't say that."

"I feel it in my bones. Yesterday, a cup slipped from my hand and when I tried to bend over to pick it up, I couldn't. There was this excruciating pain in my waist. It was so painful,

I had to call Joanna to help me pick it up. We will not be here for her forever," Babula said.

I buried myself in my new books. When I ran out of books to read, I reread the ones that Mr. Vasilli had given me. Those books took me to places I couldn't imagine myself ever being. I learned about other places in Poland and about other countries in Europe. It was exciting to know things that others my age, especially Aleksander, didn't know.

Aleksander hated the fact that I spent more time reading than playing with him. On the hill, I lay on the ground with a book held above my face. Aleksander lay beside me, doing nothing.

"I'm busy, Aleks. I don't have time to play today."

"You are always busy these days and it's not fair!" he said.

"Have you heard about Jan Brzechwa?" I asked, thrusting the book at him. "You would like it. Should we read the book together?"

"It's boring," he said.

"It's not boring!"

"It is boring."

"How do you know that? You haven't read the book yet, so how can you say that?" I asked.

"I don't need to read the book to know what it's about. Let's play the guessing game instead."

"I want to read my book."

"But you have read the book over and over again!" he cried.

"Yes! Because it is interesting. There is so much to learn from this book. Did you know that London is in England?"

"Yes!" he said as he stuck out his tongue.

"Liar! You didn't know that, but now you know, thanks to me."

"Did you learn that from this book?" he asked.

"No. I got that from the other books I have read," I answered.

He snatched the book from me and I cried out.

"What are you doing?" I asked.

"What does it look like I am doing?"

"That's not funny! I want my book back!"

"But it's not yours. It belongs to Mr. Vasilli," he said.

"Mr. Vasilli gave the book to me, so now it belongs to me!" I said.

Suddenly, he bolted for a tree. I ran after him.

"Stop! Stop it now, Aleks!" I cried out.

He grabbed a branch and pulled himself up. Looking down at me, he said, "The first person to get to the top of the tree keeps the book."

I jumped up and grabbed a branch, then hoisted myself up with a push. I rested my left foot on one branch and my right foot on another. I gripped another branch for support. My hands and legs hurt and I was exhausted. Branch by branch, I climbed the tree. When I looked up, Aleksander was already at the top.

"I get to keep the book," he said as he grinned.

I was worn out by the time I climbed down from the tree.

"I know what you did," I said when he got down from the tree.

"What did I do?"

"You are not going to take the book."

"Why do you say that?" he asked.

"Because I know you so well. You are not going to read the book and your brothers would probably throw it away."

"I will read it."

"Liar!" I said.

"I swear, I will read it, and then I will tell you about it."

"You are lying. You will not open the book."

He touched his belly as he burst into laughter. "Of course I wasn't going to read the book. I just wanted to have fun and I did. We climbed the tree today and today wasn't boring!"

"I knew you were not going to read the book!" I said as I joined in the laughter.

In August, we received a second letter from my father. We were all excited to read it. Babula sat on the edge of

Grandfather's bed while I stood in front of them, reading out the letter.

Warsaw,

August 15, 1939.

My dearest Joanna,

Thankfully, I received your letter, but I didn't get it right away. Hence, the reason why my reply is coming late. Your baba is fine and doing well. How is everyone back at home? How are Babula and your grandfather? How is Jasper? Is he still alive? I miss you all so much. I cannot wait to hold you in my arms and kiss you goodnight. It has been only a few months but it feels like I haven't seen everyone in years. You should have grown taller now and your hair should be longer now. Oh, and more beautiful, too!

I miss your grandfather so much. Tell him I miss our discussions. Yes, things are getting pretty serious here. Rumors are flying around that the Germans might come for Poland. God forbid the Germans invade Poland, baba, I might have to go to war! I pray this won't happen.

Joanna, my dearest, I want you to be strong and take care of your grandparents. Don't run off and be naughty.

Your grandparents are getting old and they need all the assistance they can get. Be nice to them and be obedient.

There are so many things I want to say, but time will not permit it. I have just a few minutes to write this and give the letter to the person who will help me post it to you.

I miss everyone and I hope to see you soon!

With love,
Your baba,
Filip.

Babula insisted that we write to him immediately.

Kalusyn,
August 15, 1939

Dear Baba,

I wish you well, baba. Everyone at home is safe and we are happy that all is well with you. Shavuot wasn't fun without you. And Babula wants me to report myself to you. She's mad at me because I snuck out during Torah. How was Shavuot over there? Were you allowed to observe it? Everything has been fine here and we all miss you.

Babula is not as strong as she used to be. She can no longer bend her knees. These days, I am the one helping them walk around. It is not easy, but I can manage. I am grown now and I have more responsibilities.

I have a new friend and Aleksander is jealous. His name is Mr. Vasilli. Well, he is not really my friend because he is older than me. He just moved here with his family to teach at the elementary school and he gave me some of his sons' old books. I have been busy lately, reading books and getting enough knowledge about things. Now, I can join you and Grandfather in your discussions about the government.

Do you know about Jan Brzechwa? Have you heard of him? I have read his book and I can say that I have found my inspiration. I think I know what I will become in the future. I want to become a writer. I've told Babula and Grandfather about it and they love the idea. One day, I will write about you, Babula, and grandfather!

Jasper is fine. I can't wait for you to see him when you come back. He has grown and is quite different from the Jasper you gave me before you left.

We miss you, baba!

With love,

Grandpa, Babula, and Joanna.

My father's letter brought a bit of comfort to us. I kept the letter, placing it in a small wooden box containing the other letter he had written.

Babula spent most of her time sitting, as her knees were getting bad. I helped her around the house and to the Shul. After a few days, she could no longer go to the Shul. It was disheartening to see my grandparents that way. Babula wasn't as agile as she used to be. Now she sat in the kitchen and gave me instructions on what to cut and put into the pot. I started doing things that I hadn't been doing before. Aunt Maja was right! I should have learned some of those things long ago.

It wasn't easy, but I couldn't complain. It was my turn to be there for them, the way they had been there for me when my mama passed away. My grandfather had said that he and Babula had to move into my father's house so that they could be there for me.

"She needs a woman's presence in the house," my grandfather had said. "Except if you want to get married again. Do you want to?" he asked my father.

He shook his head. "Joanna took half of the love left in me to the grave. The remaining love I have is for my daughter and no other woman."

It had been my father's idea that I be named after my mama.

"I don't think that's a good idea," Babula had said.

"Why not?" he asked.

"She already looks so much like Joanna. Now you want to name her Joanna, too?"

"Is that a bad thing?" my father asked.

"It is terrible! How can you move on?!"

"I will move on, but I want her to have that name! It means so much to me."

———————

Aleksander got over his fear of dogs. Throughout the months, he fell in love with Jasper. With Babula and my grandfather not as strong as they used to be, he came over to help me take care of them.

"I was wrong about your friend," Babula had said. "He has a kind soul. It might be difficult to find someone else like him. He reminds me so much of Maja. I guess I might see her sooner than I think."

Fear gripped me whenever Babula spoke like that. She always found a way to turn our discussions to death and how I should be prepared to take charge of things in case she fell asleep and didn't wake up.

I found comfort in reading my father's letters. I looked forward to receiving them and hoped that he would write to us soon. However, August 1939 was the last time we heard from my father. In the months to come, things took a turn and Kaluszyn witnessed the other side of life.

ANNA DRAZEK

BOOK TWO

ANNA DRAZEK

CHAPTER SEVEN

September 1939

A dark shadow enveloped Poland from the first of September 1939, and it extracted every iota of happiness in everyone. On the second of September, someone knocked on our door and I jerked out of bed. Jasper walked into my room, wagging his tail. We dashed to the living room. Before I opened the door, my grandfather called out my name. I left the living room and went to his room, then hurried to his bedside.

"I heard a noise. Is someone at the door?" he asked.

"Yes, someone's at the door," I replied.

"Isn't it too early for someone to be at the door? Who is it? Is it Aleksander?"

"I don't know yet," I said. Jasper licked my finger and I pushed him away gently.

"Alright, go and find out," my grandfather said.

"I'll be right back!" I said. I left the room. Jasper walked behind me.

"Be careful!" my grandfather said.

I hurried to the door. "Is that you, Aleks?"

"No! Open up! It's me, Vasilli," a voice called from outside.

I unbolted the door and Mr. Vasilli barged into the house with his youngest son, Stefan. He panted heavily as he looked at me. It was early in the morning and sweat had already gathered on his forehead.

"I need to speak to your grandparents," he said. "Are they in?"

I nodded.

"Tell them it's urgent," Mr. Vasilli said.

"Okay, sir," I said. I wondered what was so important that he had come to our house a few minutes before seven in the morning. "I'll be right back. I walked slowly to my grandfather's room, then kneeled beside his bed. I tapped him gently. My grandfather opened his eyes. Babula appeared at the door.

"What's going on?" she asked, walking into the room with a walking stick.

I ran to her and wrapped my arms around her waist.

"What are you doing, Babula? You shouldn't be out of bed without my help," I said.

"I thought I heard something. What's going on? Was someone at the door?" Babula said.

"It's Mr. Vasilli and his son, Stefan," I said as I guided her to the bed. She sat on it and touched my grandfather's hand.

"Good morning," Babula said.

"Good morning," my grandfather replied.

"Joanna, what do Mr. Vasilli and his son want with us?" my grandfather said.

"I don't know," I responded. "He said he wanted to speak to you and Babula. He said it is urgent."

My grandparents shared a look. Then my grandfather said, "Bring them here."

I led Mr. Vasilli and Stefan to my grandfather's room.

"Good morning," Mr. Vasilli and Stefan said in unison.

"Good morning," Babula replied. Grandfather replied a few seconds later.

"I'm sorry to bother everyone this early in the morning, but I had to come down here."

"What's the matter?" my grandfather asked.

"We found some strangers in town this morning," Mr. Vasilli said.

"Strangers?" my grandfather asked.

"Yes, refugees. They ran away from Warsaw because the Germans have invaded there."

Dead silence filled the room. I didn't know how to react to what Mr. Vasilli had said. Then, I looked at my grandparents. Babula looked petrified, but I couldn't tell how my grandfather felt. Finally, I walked toward the bed and sat on it. Jasper strolled into the room and approached me. I put him on my lap.

"When was that?" my grandfather asked.

"It started yesterday morning. Many people from Warsaw are trooping into Kaluszyn as I speak."

"What about France? What about Great Britain? Are they coming? Are they helping?" my grandfather asked.

"There has been radio silence from them," Mr. Vasilli replied.

"Do you think the war will get here?" Babula asked.

"The war will reach everywhere," Stefan said. "Hitler's plan is to control all of Europe, so I don't think Kaluszyn is off-limits. Kaluszyn isn't safe anymore. The best thing is to get prepared and-"

"Get prepared for what?" Babula asked.

"Get prepared to leave. I'm taking my family away from Kaluszyn. I don't know what will happen if we remain here and I don't want to find out!" Mr. Vasilli said.

"Where will you go?" my grandfather asked.

"Anywhere but here. I think you should do the same," Mr. Vasilli said as he turned to me. "Have you heard from your father?"

I shook my head.

"He will be fighting the German army, so I don't think he will have time to send letters," Stefan said.

"We think you all should come with us," Mr. Vasilli said.

"All of us?" my grandfather asked.

"Yes," Mr. Vasilli said.

"Joanna will go with you alone," my grandfather said.

"No!" I said. "I'm not leaving my grandparents behind."

Babula caressed my face. "We are not healthy enough to come along."

"What if my baba comes back home?"

"Your father can't-"

"He might! He might come back home to protect us!" I said as I tried to stifle my tears. "I don't want to leave you behind. Who will take care of you and Grandfather? If I leave Kaluszyn, you might never see me again. What about my baba? What if he comes back home and I am not here to welcome him?"

Mr. Vasilli got down on one knee and touched my hands. "Your father enlisted in the army, Joanna. This is the time the country needs him most. He can't come back now."

I couldn't hold back anymore. My body trembled as gut-wrenching tears gushed out of my eyes. "Why not?" I choked out.

"He's fighting in the war. Your father is brave to defend Poland. All you have to do right now is be brave for your grandparents," Mr. Vasilli said.

"I...I...I," I stammered. Tears had clogged my vision. I wiped my face with my palms. "What about Aleks? I don't want to go anywhere without him. He's the only friend I have."

"It's okay. It's okay. My wife will be there to take care of you. Also, you can bring your books so that you will have something to read whenever you're bored," Mr. Vasilli said.

"I'm not sure about all this," I said.

"When do you intend to leave?" my grandfather asked.

"Very soon, but I need to contact some friends and family before we set out," Mr. Vasilli said.

"It's settled, then. Joanna will go with you," my grandfather said.

"I don't-"

"It's for the best!" my grandfather said. "Come...come over here."

I crawled onto the bed and sat next to him.

"It's for the best," he said.

I sniffed. "But-"

"Your Babula and I are not as strong as we used to be. It would be a major setback for everyone if we followed Mr. Vasilli and his family. Don't worry. They are nice people and will take good care of you. Don't worry about Babula and me. We will be fine. If everything goes well, you can always come back. Write a letter to your father and leave it somewhere in the house, a place you know he will see it. Tell him you have left with Mr. Vasilli and that you are fine. Forget about Aleksander. He has his family to protect him. Now you have Mr. Vasilli and his family to protect you," My grandfather said.

I hugged him and burst into uncontrollable tears.

———————

In the afternoon, Aleksander came to help me take care of my grandparents. After washing them with washcloths soaked in warm water, we sat on the floor. I hugged my knees as tears flowed down my cheeks. Jasper growled, pulling on my dress.

"Leave my dress alone, Jasper!" I said.

He whirled around and ran to me. I stretched my legs forward and crossed my ankles. He lay on my lap quietly.

"My parents are preparing to leave Kaluszyn," Aleksander said.

"For where?" I asked as I patted Jasper's head.

"We don't know yet. But I have started packing my bags. My sister doesn't want to leave yet."

"Why?" I asked.

"I'm not sure. But I think it has to do with a boy," Aleksander said.

I looked at him in disbelief. "There is war and all your sister can think about is a boy?"

He shrugged. "I don't want to leave here without you, and you don't want to leave here without me-"

"Our situation is different. We are like-"

"Twins?"

"Yes. We are like twins."

"So, will you follow Mr. Vasilli and his family?" he asked.

"I don't know yet. My grandparents think it's the right thing to do. But I don't want to leave them behind. I like Mr. Vasilli and his family. Stefan and his brother have been nice to me and they are very funny. And his wife cooks for my grandparents and me sometimes," I said.

"So, what's the problem?"

"It's going to be different. It won't be the same as it would be with family. No matter what, I will still be an outsider."

"Remember Mr. Lech and his family?"

"Yes. What about them?" I asked.

"They adopted Marian. Nobody knows Marian is adopted. I wouldn't have known if you hadn't told me, and you wouldn't have known if Babula hadn't been the one who found the boy when he was a baby."

"What's your point?"

"All I am saying is that if you go with them, they will take you into their home and treat you well. I am positive that Mr. Vasilli and his family will do that. And you will get to read so many books," Aleksander said.

"Mr. Vasilli will be with his family, and you will be with yours, Aleks. It's not as easy as you say. Wherever I go, I will be troubled because I don't know what will have become of my grandparents and baba. It won't be the same without them."

"I understand," he said.

The voices on the radio reverberated in the house.

"So, it's war!" the voices said.

"It's war," I mumbled.

There was an uproar on the streets outside the house. Aleksander flung open the window to see what was happening. He gasped. Jasper and I joined him. Outside, many men walked in masse with rucksacks, chanting and swinging their hands in the air.

"What's happening?" I asked.

"I think they want to go and fight in the war," Aleksander replied.

I faced him. "Are you serious?"

"Yes."

"They might never come back."

"Someone has to defend us," he said.

"Like my baba."

"Yes, like him."

We whirled around as we heard the sound of bombs and people shouting on the radio. The speaker said, "Run! They are approaching! Pack your-"

I shivered. Aleksander held my hand and smiled. "Nothing bad will happen to us, I promise."

CHAPTER EIGHT

S oon, food became a luxury. The markets and food shops were almost empty, as only a few peasants brought their produce to the market. The population in Kaluszyn had tripled, with anxious people flocking there from Warsaw. Aleksander and I waited at the railway station, hoping my father would return from Warsaw. In all our lives in Kaluszyn, we had never seen the station as crowded as it was that day. A huge crowd flocked in and out, and it was difficult for Aleksander and me to hear what each other was saying because the voices of others drowned out ours. Aleksander held my hand tightly as he pulled me through the crowd of people. I could hear the echoes of children as they called out to their parents.

"Mama!" a small girl called out. She stood close to us.

"She can't find her mama," I said.

"What?" Aleksander asked as he leaned toward me.

I pointed to the girl. "I said she can't find her mama."

He looked at the little girl for a moment. Then he looked at me.

"She's like me. She's looking for her mama and I am looking for my baba," I said.

A hand pulled the little girl away from us.

We spent an hour at the station. There was no sign of my father. Then we sat under a tree a few steps from the station.

"Should we go back home?" Aleksander asked.

I shook my head. "No!"

"I don't think he is coming back."

"You don't know that," I said.

"If he comes back from Warsaw, he will come home immediately," he said.

"But I want to be right here when he comes back!"

"We can't continue to do this, Joanna!" Aleksander said.

"You don't have to wait with me."

"You know I won't leave here without you," he said.

I kept silent.

"Fine. What about your grandparents? You can't leave them alone in the house," he said.

"I will leave them eventually, right? That's what everyone is saying," I said.

"What are you talking about?" he asked.

"You want me to leave with Mr. Vasilli, and my grandparents think it's for the best, too. So, you see, I'm going to leave them eventually. I might as well start now."

I looked away as my face turned red. My eyes were wet with tears.

"Let's go back home, Joanna," he said.

"Give me a minute," I said.

––––––––

I heard the voices on the radio no matter where I went in Kaluszyn. Everyone had their radios turned on to keep up with the war. My grandfather made sure the radio was turned on every single day. I wrung the water out of the washcloth and wiped his right hand. The man on the radio was talking about the bombing of the railway station in Mrozy.

"What does that mean?" I asked as I wiped his left hand. His eyes were fixed on the ceiling and his lips were pressed together.

"What does that mean?" I asked again.

He grunted and his eyes widened.

"Many things," he said. "Many bad things, Joanna. It's a pity you have to witness this war. It's a pity!"

We didn't speak to each other again until I dumped the washcloth into the bowl and stood up from the bed.

"Where are you going?" he asked.

"To wash Babula."

"Hmm-mmm. How is she doing?" he asked.

"She's not bad," I replied.

"Can she walk on her own?"

"Not really," I said.

"I would like to speak to her," My grandfather said.

"I will bring her after I finish washing her. I heard on the radio that they have bombed most of the schools in Warsaw. They have killed the professors and-"

"Don't worry about the news on the radio. Just pack your things so that you can leave with Mr. Vasilli and his family when they are ready," he said.

I nodded and stepped out of the room.

Our rabbi had asked every one of us to come to the Shul to help serve soup and bread to the Jewish refugees. The Shul was packed with so many refugees that there was barely enough space to walk around. Mats were spread on the floor, holding mostly women and their children. The cries of babies and little children pierced the atmosphere. Blood was smeared on their faces and bodies. Nurses and doctors tended to the injured. Their faces were covered with grief. I had not seen what they had seen back in Warsaw, but somehow I could feel their pain. Many of them had lost family members. Some didn't know where their children or husbands or wives were.

I stopped in front of a man who sat in a corner. He looked up at me. His right eye was closed and black all over. His left eye was barely open.

"I brought soup," I said.

He collected the soup with trembling hands, then shoved it down his throat.

"Thank you," he said as he returned the empty bowl. His voice was scratchy like a grater was stuck in his throat.

I walked back to the temporary kitchen that had been set up outside the Shul to take care of the refugees. A woman ran past me with a baby in her arms.

"He's not breathing," she kept saying.

The nurses took the baby from her hands.

"He's dead," one of the nurses whispered to the others.

"Are you sure?"

"Check him."

"Is he dead?" the mother asked. "Why is my baby not breathing? Is my son dead? He can't be dead, right? He was alive in Warsaw and on the train."

"He's dead," one of the nurses said.

"I breastfed him this morning. He…he was…alive. He was alive!" the mother said.

"I'm sorry, he's dead," another nurse said.

"His father was shot. I can't lose him, too," the woman said.

Aleksander returned with a basket full of empty dishes. He glanced at the woman and the nurses as he walked past them.

"What happened to her?" he asked.

"Her baby is dead."

There was a brief silence. Then Aleksander dropped the basket and held my hands in his.

"Your baba is fine, wherever he is," he said.

Aleksander always knew the right words to say, whether I was sad or happy. It saddened me that I would be apart from my family and Aleksander because of Hitler. Whenever they spoke about the war, my father and grandfather never said anything good about Hitler.

"He is a madman," my father had said.

"A real madman," my grandfather said.

"He wants to dominate everywhere. Imagine!" my father said.

"As if we haven't suffered enough, he wants us to suffer more."

"But we have France and Britain at our backs if he tries anything funny," my father said.

"The British and French could be very funny, too," my grandfather said. "Only Poland can't be funny to Poland."

THE OTHER SIDE OF LIFE

The woman fell to the ground, cuddling her dead baby and sobbing quietly. The nurses had left her alone as they tended to other sick and injured refugees.

"I can't imagine what she must be going through. First, her husband was shot, and now her baby is dead. That's so sad," I said.

"I don't know what I would do if I lost my family," Aleksander said. "As annoying as they are, I wouldn't trade them for anyone else."

A girl came out of the Shul and walked up to us. She was the same height as me, and I could tell that we were the same age. Her scraggly blond hair looked like a dirty mop. Her forehead was stained with sand, and her nails were black with dirt. She waved at us.

"Hello," she said.

"Hello," we replied.

"Please, we need water," she said. "My brother and I are thirsty."

"We've run out of water," I said.

"Thanks anyway," she said as she whirled around.

"Wait!" I said on impulse. "What's your name?"

"Julia."

"I'm Joanna. I don't live far from here. There's water back at home," I said.

I took Julia and her brother, Lech, back to the house while Aleksander stayed behind. They drank clean water and had a bath. I helped Julia brush her hair in my room.

"What's your dog's name?" Julia asked.

"Jasper," I said as I glanced over my shoulder. Jasper lay on the bed, watching us. "It's just you and your brother?"

"Yes."

I wanted to ask about her parents, but I didn't.

"We don't know where they are," she said.

"What?" I asked.

"Our parents. There was shooting and bombing. We had to leave. What about you?" she asked.

"What about me?" I said as I packed her hair into a high bun.

"You and your brother live with your grandparents alone?" she asked.

"Brother?" I asked.

"Yes, that boy at the Shul."

"Oh no, Aleks is not my brother. I mean, he is like my brother but-my...I'm sorry," I said. "My grandparents live with my baba and me."

"Where is he?" she asked.

"Who?" I asked.

"Your baba."

"He is fighting in the war," I said. "He left me with Jasper before he left."

Lech stood at the door.

"It's okay," I said. "You can come in."

"How old are you?" Julia asked.

"I'm nine. You?" I asked.

"I will be eleven in December. Lech is five."

Lech sat on the bed. He tickled Jasper, who rolled on the bed.

"Thank you," Julia said as she looked in the mirror. "I look like a normal person now."

I had given her one of my dresses, and Lech was wearing some of Jan's clothes.

"Can your grandparents walk?" she asked.

"My grandpa can't walk, but my Babula can manage a little. Why?" I asked.

"What if the German soldiers come here? I heard some women say something like that."

"I hope not. I don't want to think about that."

"My brother and I plan on leaving," she said.

"Where will you go?" I asked.

"We don't know. Back at the Shul, some refugees were talking about leaving. Maybe we would go with them."

"Are you sure you want to leave with them?"

"We followed some people from Warsaw when we overhead them talking about leaving for Kaluszyn. I don't think it's wise to stay in one place. Kaluszyn is not safe. They can come here anytime," she said.

"What about our soldiers? Weren't they of any help?" I asked.

Julia shook her head. "I don't know about anyone. There were shootings and bombings everywhere. It was scary! Nobody came to help us. We had to help ourselves."

"My grandparents want me to leave with a family," I said. "They are nice people and they will take care of me."

"That's for the best. The German soldiers are capturing Jews," she said.

"Why?" I asked.

"They don't like us."

"I hear some sounds in the night," I said.

"What sounds?" she asked.

"I don't know how to explain it, but whenever I hear it, it's from the sky-"

Almost immediately, she said, "German planes!"

"German planes?" I responded.

"Yeah, and I saw the planes, too. They were shooting from everywhere. Nowhere is safe, Joanna. If you have seen the planes too, that means nobody is safe in Kaluszyn. It's just a matter of time before they start capturing and killing people.

Trust me when I say you don't want to be here when that happens."

"My grandparents-"

"If you leave early, you can take them with you," she said.

"They can't walk properly," I said.

"Find a way."

Later that day, Aleksander and I showed Julia and her brother around the town. It was not as fun as it would have been if fewer people were there. Then, we took them to the hill and lay there in peace and quiet. Our safe place was still safe, as nobody had discovered it yet. Kaluszyn looked completely different when viewed from the hill. It looked foreign to me as I leaned against a tree and watched people who looked like tiny ants moving about.

CHAPTER NINE

We volunteered to wash the dirty plates with some other children at the Shul. Two big bowls had been placed on the ground: one for washing the dirty plates and the other for rinsing the washed plates. Aleksander and Julia washed the dirty plates with four other children while I rinsed the plates with two other girls. Lech stayed back at the house with Babula and Grandfather. No one was in the mood to say anything, as we were all preoccupied with our thoughts. The temporary kitchen was deafening with the cries and voices of people. As we washed the dirty plates, other volunteers kept dropping dirty plates and cups into the bowls.

Someone tapped me, and I turned around.

"Joanna," the man said. His lips curved into a smile as he wrapped his arms around me. "You shouldn't be here. You should be with your grandparents."

"I want to help," I said a little louder than normal so that he could hear me amid the voices that flew around.

"That's very kind of you," Mr. Henryk said. My father and Mr. Henryk had worked in the same Tallit factory before my father joined the army.

"Thank you, sir," I said.

"Have you gotten any food to eat?" Mr. Henryk asked.

I nodded.

"If you need anything, don't hesitate to-"

"Mr. Henryk?!" Another man called out his name, beckoning to him. Mr. Henryk left and walked over to the man. I bent over the bowl and continued rinsing in silence. However, I couldn't focus on the plates. I kept throwing glances at the man and Mr. Henryk. Two nurses walked over to them and whispered in their ears, then walked away. Mr. Henryk and the man walked to the back of the Shul. I wiped my hands on my damp dress.

"Where are you going?" Aleksander asked.

"I'll be right back," I said.

I followed the men to the back of the Shul. They were walking toward the farm located there. Four men were carrying a bier as they walked toward Mr. Henryk and the other man. Our rabbi walked out of the farm and beckoned to the men.

"Over here," our rabbi said. "We will bury them over there."

I moved closer so that I could see what was going on. Other men carrying biers approached the farm. The handle slipped from one of their hands and the bier came crashing down. A man fell from the bier and rolled, then stopped in front of me. I froze and my face paled. This was the first time in my life that I had seen the face of a dead man. The men quickly picked up the dead body and placed it back on the bier.

Our rabbi turned around and saw me. He called out my name before I could run back to the kitchen.

He ran toward me. "You!"

"Sir!"

"What are you doing here? You shouldn't be here!" he said.

I felt a bit disoriented as the face of the dead man clogged my mind. At that moment, it was impossible to un-see what I had already seen. I opened my mouth to speak, but no words came out.

"You shouldn't be here," he repeated.

Mr. Henryk ran toward us.

"I'll take her away from here. This is Filip Bach's daughter. Rosalia and Batos Bach's granddaughter," Mr. Henryk said.

"My good Lord! I didn't know she was the one. You shouldn't be here right now. This is for grown-ups. Go on! Go back home," our rabbi said.

Mr. Henryk held my hands and we walked back to the kitchen.

"Are you burying those men on the farm?" I asked.

"Joanna-"

"It's okay, you can tell me. I'll probably see more dead bodies during this war anyway," I said.

"They are people who died on their way here, and those who died when they got here," he replied.

"A woman was crying the other day when her baby died. Was the baby buried there, too?"

He shook his head. "I don't know. Many have lost their babies, Joanna. Enough questions. I think it's best that you and your friends go back home now."

At home, I struggled to sleep as I lay on the mat on the floor in my room. Julia and her brother slept on my bed. I kept thinking about the dead man I had seen earlier and all the dead people who were buried on the farm. Each time I shut my eyes, I pictured the dead man's face vividly. I remembered his missing left hand.

Quietly, I stood up and left the room, then entered my grandfather's room. He lay on the bed, sleeping quietly. I stepped out and went to Babula's room. I stood at the door for a while before she called my name.

"You can't sleep?" she asked.

"Yes, I can't sleep. What about you? I thought you were asleep."

"No, I couldn't sleep, either. Come over here," Babula said.

I entered the room and sat on her bed. She held my hand and smiled.

"What's wrong?" she asked.

"I saw a dead body today."

There was a brief moment of silence, followed by a chuckle.

"It's not funny, Babula," I said.

"You are right, it's not funny. I don't know why I laughed."

"Have you seen a dead body before?" I asked.

"Yes," she said.

"When was that?"

"I saw a dead body for the first time when I was six," Babula said.

"My goodness, what happened?" I asked.

"It was at the market. I can't remember how the chaos started. All I can remember was that some men were shooting everywhere. I ran into an open shop and slammed the door shut. I whirled around and slipped. I fell on a woman lying on the floor. I apologized and stood up immediately."

"What did the woman say?" I asked.

"Nothing. At first, I hadn't realized that the woman lying on the floor was dead. I couldn't scream because I was scared and the shootings were still going on outside. I hid under the table in the shop and waited for a while until the shootings stopped."

"I can't believe you stayed in the same place with a dead person for a long time," I said. "Weren't you scared?"

"I was more scared of getting shot that day. Then the gunshots stopped. When I was sure it was safe outside, I ran out of the shop. I didn't look at the dead people on the ground as I ran back home. I didn't even have the time or luxury to think about the dead woman until a few days later," Babula said.

"What happened a few days later?" I asked.

"I couldn't sleep, I couldn't eat. I couldn't do anything at all!"

"Why?" I asked. My curiosity tugged at me.

"I kept seeing the dead woman everywhere I went," Babula said.

"How did you get over it?" I asked.

"It wasn't easy, but I did."

"How?" I asked.

"I don't know, Joanna. I just did!" she said as she held my hands. My fear disappeared that night as I lay on the bed next to Babula. I shut my eyes and slept like a baby.

The number of refugees who came to Kaluszyn had tripled. As people were leaving Kaluszyn, others were arriving. Nobody knew what they were doing or where they were going. I had packed my bags and was waiting for Mr. Vasilli and his family to let me know when they were leaving. Aleksander and his family were leaving soon, and Julia and her brother would be leaving with some other refugees in a few days. There was not enough food and water in Kaluszyn, and everyone, including the refugees, was starving.

Aleksander and I spent most of our time volunteering at the Shul. There was not enough to go around, so food and water had to be rationed. I made sure I got enough food for Babula and Grandfather whenever I volunteered at the Shul. Mats and foams were no longer available and the refugees had to lie on the cold ground. The Shul, schools, and streets were filled with people. Julia and Lech stayed in my house, as other homes in Kaluszyn had to house refugees because of overpopulation.

Nine days after the war broke out, there was not enough to feed everyone, as the bakers had run out of flour. The following day, everyone had to line up at the only bakery in town that still had bread. After getting our portion, we went back to my house to feed Babula and Grandfather.

"When are you leaving?" Babula asked as she ate the bread slowly, sitting beside my grandfather on the bed.

"Mr. Vasilli said tomorrow or the day after."

"Where are you going?" she asked.

"I'm not sure yet. He said we will go to Morozi or Dobri first because his mother lives in Dobri and he has a sister in Morozi."

"That's good," my grandfather said. "You've packed your bags?"

"Yes, Grandfather."

Tears escaped Babula's eyes. "I can't believe this is happening. I love you so much and your baba would be proud of you, wherever he is."

Tears formed in my eyes and I fought to control them.

"I'll miss you and grandfather," I said.

Later in the day, I sat at the desk in my room while Juliet and her brother slept on the bed. I wrote to my father in the hope that he would read the letter someday.

Kaluszyn,
September 9, 1939

Dear Baba,

I am writing this letter in the hope that you get to hold and read it. I hope that you are doing well and that you are still alive. Jasper and I are leaving town with Mr. Vasilli and his family tomorrow or the day after. We are going to Morozi or Dobri. His mother lives in Dobri and he has a sister in Morozi. We will stay there for a while as Mr. Vasilli considers what to do next. It saddens my heart that Babula and Grandfather cannot come with us. I know I will be lonely without them, but I will be strong for you, Grandfather, and Babula.

We ate the last bread in Kaluszyn today and nobody knows what will happen tomorrow. Baba, you wouldn't believe what has become of Kaluszyn. There are refugees everywhere, and everywhere has now become a refugee camp. Oh, there's a girl and her brother staying with us now. Her name is Julia and her brother is Lech. We met them at the Shul where Aleksander and I have been volunteering.

I wish you were here with us, baba. Don't get killed, and continue to fight off the enemy. If you ever get to read this letter, please look for me, baba.

I love you so much, baba!

With love,

Joanna

I folded the letter and left it on the desk. In the evening, Stefan came over to tell my grandparents that they were leaving Kaluszyn for Dobri the following day. I spent the night packing the rest of my things into a rucksack. Julia and her brother decided to accompany us to Dobri. Aleksander and his family were leaving two days later. He spent the night and none of us could get any sleep. We talked about everything we could remember about Kaluszyn and how we were going to miss it.

"I'll miss the Shul," Aleksander said.

"What do you mean you will miss the Shul?" I asked.

"Well, just because I never enjoyed attending the Shul doesn't mean that I'm not going to miss it. Many things happened at the Shul!"

My eyes crinkled at the corners as I burst into laughter. Julia and Lech laughed hysterically. Jasper barked as if he understood what we were talking about.

"What do you mean many things happened at the Shul?" Julia asked, her voice choked with laughter.

"Actually," I said, chuckling. "Many fun things happened at the Shul!"

"Do you remember when our rabbi chased us into the Shul?" Aleksander asked.

"He chased us into the Shul many times, Aleks. If he didn't chase us, my Babula would chase us!"

Our laughter continued, bursting from deep within us.

CHAPTER TEN

September 10, 1939 was the day we were supposed to leave town. We were on Kościelna Street, trying to get water into our flask so that we wouldn't get thirsty during our journey. Many people had left Kaluszyn the previous day, and many were leaving that day. We had spent a little over an hour in the queue at the water pump. Lech played with the other kids while Aleksander, Julia, and I remained in the queue. I could feel an overwhelming pain in my heart. I was leaving Kaluszyn without my family, and all I wanted to do was cry. However, I had to suppress my tears because I didn't want to cry in public.

Suddenly, someone screamed, and everyone looked in the direction of the noise.

"Run! Run! Run!" a boy yelled as he ran toward the queue.

I whirled around in confusion. "What's going on?" I asked Aleksander.

A woman knocked me down in an attempt to carry her child. A man stepped on my chest as he tried to jump over my body. Aleksander helped me to my feet, but within a fraction of a second, I heard a blast that threw me back to the ground. My eyes rolled around in the darkness that had overshadowed everything. A fire broke out in some of the houses around the water pump. Voices floated in the air, and I heard the roaring scream of people coming from everywhere. Many people were on the ground, seriously hurt. My strength waned as I tried to get to my feet, but I couldn't stand. I squinted to look around but everything was blurry. I could feel myself slowly drifting away into a sinister place devoid of light.

I must have blacked out for hours. When I woke, I tasted sand mixed with blood. My eyelids slowly fluttered open and I squinted at the sparkling light that flooded my eyes. I looked to my right and then to my left. Fear gripped me. I tried to steady my breath, as my anxiety was already giving way to panic. Then, a foot stopped directly in front of my line of sight. It belonged to a short man. He pulled me up gently and stared directly into my eyes.

"Are you alright?" he asked. "Can you talk?"

"Yes...yes," I stammered as I spat on the ground.

Pain surged through my left leg. I tried to move, then fell into his arms.

"I...I can't move," I said.

"Someone here is injured!" the short man yelled. "We need help here!"

A man rushed toward me and told me to sit back on the ground. He looked like a healthcare worker. People were choking and blubbering around me. I looked at my leg and gasped at the magma-red blood spurting from it.

"You're going to be fine," the short man said as he placed his hands on my shoulders.

"What happened?" I asked. "What happened?"

"There was a bomb," the healthcare worker said. "We're going to carry you and put you on a bier. It's going to be painful at first-"

"Where're you taking me?" I asked.

"To the camp. Your leg needs to be treated," the nurse replied. "I'm Nowak, and you will be fine."

My body shook with a memory I was trying to forget. I looked around and my fear spiked.

"Where is Aleks?" I asked.

"Aleks who?" the short man and Nowak asked in unison.

"My friend. And Lech and Julia? Where are they? We were standing together when...when...But, please, where are my friends? Are they alive?"

"What's your name?" Nowak asked.

"I'm Joanna. Filip Bach is my father."

"We will contact your father," the short man said.

"No!" I said. "My father is fighting in the war. I live with my grandparents, Rosalia and Batos Bach."

"Enough talking now," the short man said. Nowak pulled a bier close to me, and they picked me up and put me on it. I lay like the dead men on it back at the Shul.

"My friends!" I said as the short man wheeled me away. It felt like I was passing through a graveyard, and my stomach clenched. Lifeless bodies were lying on the ground. Blood was everywhere, and the smell of smoke lingered in the air.

"Are you going to find my friends?" I asked again.

The short man stopped and leaned toward me.

"Okay, what are their names?" he asked.

"Aleksander Malinowski, Lech, and Julia. I don't know their last names."

He nodded, then lifted the bier and continued wheeling me to the camp. When we got there, I was lifted and placed on a bed. Every minute, a horde of people was rushed into the room, crying and moaning. The person beside me was wrapped in bandages from head to toe, and she kept screaming in pain. Activity buzzed around me. The room smelled of blood, sweat, alcohol, and bleach.

"I can't find my daughter!" a patient cried out.

"My head hurts!" another patient cried out.

The patient on the bed opposite me vomited. I looked away immediately. Soon, two ladies came to my bed and tended to my wounds.

When I woke up later in the evening, the room was filled with patients. I had a slight throbbing pain in my head, and the nurses said they had run out of medications. Vomit hung in my throat, and I felt like I might throw up. The smell in the room choked me, and I wanted to get out of there. I sat on the bed and placed my bandaged leg on the floor.

"Excuse me," I called out to a woman who walked past my bed, but she didn't look at me.

People walked past quickly. It seemed like most of us were invisible.

"Hello," I said. I grabbed a man's hands as he hurried past my bed.

"How can I help you?" he asked.

"I…I'm thirsty," I said. "I need water."

"She needs water!" he yelled, then walked away.

A young woman walked over and gave me a cup of water. She left before I could thank her.

I stood up and staggered toward the exit door. Then I whirled around and started looking for my friends. They were not in the room, so I walked out. Nobody called me back, and nobody noticed I was leaving.

A similar sight greeted me outside the room. People lay on the ground under tents while nurses and doctors ran around, tending to them. I inspected the patients, but none of them were my friends.

"Hello," I said to a woman. "I'm looking for my friends. Aleksander, Lech, and Julia."

She shook her head. "I'm sorry, I don't know who they are."

"Okay, thank you."

I walked away from the tent.

———————

Julia and her brother weren't there when I got home.

"Julia!" I called out. "Lech! Lech!"

There was no answer. Then, Jasper barked as he ran toward me. I sat on the chair in the living room and let him lick my hands.

"I'm injured, Jasper," I told him. "There was a bomb and I was injured. Have you seen Lech, Julia, and Aleks?"

Jasper continued to lick my hand.

"Babula! Grandpa!" I yelled.

"Joanna!" my grandfather called out. "Joanna!"

I entered his room with Jasper.

"Have you seen Julia and Lech?" I asked.

"The house has been so silent since you left this morning. Why are you looking for them?"

"You don't know?" I asked him.

"Know what?"

"There was an attack this morning. Some people died, while others were injured," I said as I sat on the bed.

"Are you alright? I hope nothing happened to you."

"No," I said. I didn't tell him about my injured leg because I didn't want him to worry. "I'm fine."

"You don't sound fine, Joanna. Are you sure you are telling the truth?" he asked.

"Yes, I'm telling the truth. Nothing happened to me."

"What about Mr. Vasilli? Are you not leaving today?" he asked.

I had forgotten all about Mr. Vasilli and our journey.

"I don't know," I said.

"Go to their house and find out. You can't stay here any longer. If there was a bomb attack today, we don't know what will become of everyone tomorrow," my grandfather said.

I was dizzy from the pain in my leg, but I managed to walk to Mr. Vasilli's house. I knocked continuously on their door, but nobody answered. Then, I called out his, his wife's, and his children's names, but still nobody answered the door. Finally, I touched the doorknob, and the door opened. It was unlike them to leave their house unlocked. I opened the door and placed a foot into the house.

"Mr. Vasilli?" I called out again.

"They're not here!" a voice said behind me.

I whirled around. A girl stood behind me.

"What did you say?"

"They left immediately after the bombing," she said.

"I…I don't understand."

"I saw them when they were leaving. The bombing scared them off, so they decided to leave immediately. It would be best if you left, too. Everyone is leaving. There's nothing left here for anyone," she said as she walked away.

I didn't know how to react to what she told me. It felt like I was dreaming and everything would be okay when I woke up. However, it wasn't a dream. I was in pain, my grandparents were bedridden, I didn't know where my father was, and there was a possibility that my friends were dead.

"Mr. Vasilli!" I yelled as I banged on the door. I didn't want to believe that it was true. I walked into their house, then leaned against the wall to steady my body. The place was in chaos. Chairs and tables were turned upside down, while papers, nylons, and bottles littered the floor.

"Mr. Vasilli!" I called out again. "Stefan! Joseph!"

Everything was falling apart. I walked out of the house, dejected. The girl was right, and I had to get out of Kaluszyn as soon as possible.

———————

"Joanna! Joanna! Joanna!"

I heard my name.

"Joanna! Joanna!"

I whirled in confusion. Lech and Aleksander ran toward me as I approached the Shul.

"Aleks! Lech!" I called out.

Our hands spread wide as we hugged each other. I staggered backward as I felt a piercing pain in my leg.

"Sorry," Lech said.

"You're hurt!" Aleksander said. "Thank God you are alive."

"You're hurt, too!" I said as I touched his bandaged hands. He winced and I apologized immediately. "I've been looking for you. Where have you been?!" I asked.

"We've been Looking for you, too!" Aleksander said.

"We went back to your house, but we couldn't find you," Lech said.

I brushed back his hair. "Me too. But my grandfather said no one came to the house."

"Your grandparents were asleep when we came. We asked around for you, but nobody could tell us anything," Aleksander said.

I looked around. "Where's Julia?"

"Over there," Lech said as he pointed to the Shul.

"She's inside. She's hurt, but she's fine."

We were not dead, but that didn't take away the fear and sadness that we felt. So many had lost their loved ones that day, and their tears pierced the atmosphere.

"They've left me behind," I said.

"Who?" Aleksander asked.

"Mr. Vasilli and his family."

"What? Are you sure?" he asked.

I nodded. "They left after the bombing."

"What will you do?" he asked.

I shook my head.

Julia was on a mat inside the Shul.

"Joanna!" she said when she saw us. "I thought you were dead. I'm so glad you're alive!"

We kneeled on the mat.

"I thought you were dead, too. How are you?" I asked.

"Not so good. My belly hurts. What about Mr. Vasilli? Shouldn't we be on our way out of here?"

"I don't think any of us is in a good position to go anywhere right now," Aleksander said.

ANNA DRAZEK

"It's just a scratch," Julia said. She pulled away the sheet, exposing her lower left tummy. A blood-stained bandage covered her wound.

"This looks bad!" I said.

"It's not that bad," Julia said. "We can still make it out of here if we leave now."

"No. We all sustained injuries except Lech," Aleksander said. "My sister is unconscious, and she's receiving treatment. We can't leave until you and her are alright to travel. And Joanna's leg hurts, too."

"I can walk. I don't care if my belly is hurting me right now. I can walk, and Lech is not injured," Julia said.

"Mr. Vasilli and his family left immediately after the bombing," I told her.

"No! No! It can't be!" she said.

"That's what I said when I found out."

"I thought the plan was to leave with us? Why would they do this?" she asked.

"I don't know. We have to find another way to leave," I said.

"You can come with us!" Aleksander said. "That would be great! I don't think my parents would have an issue with that."

"I want to leave now!" Julia said.

"I can't walk properly," I said.

"We can't stay here. What if they come back? What if the bombing was just a warning and they are coming back to finish what they started?" Julia asked.

She winced in sudden pain as she tried to stand. Aleksander reached out to her, but she smacked his hand.

"I can stand on my own. I'm fine! What happened back there is just the tip of the iceberg. I saw what they did to us in Warsaw, and I don't want to witness that again. I know we are all hurt, but promise me we will leave Kaluszyn tomorrow," Julia said.

"Yes," I said while Lech and Aleksander nodded.

———

In the middle of the night, Julia began to violently throw up. We stood outside the house, watching her vomit.

"What's wrong with her?" Lech asked, his voice reflecting fear.

"She's burning up," I replied as I touched her forehead. He touched her forehead to confirm her temperature.

"My goodness, Julia! You're burning up!" he said.

Sweat gathered on Julia's forehead and dripped down her face.

"We should have stayed back at the Shul. Now I don't know what to do," I said.

"Stay back at the Shul? We can't leave your grandparents behind," Julia said.

I shrugged. "You are not feeling well, Julia. I don't know what to do. But first, we need to get you back to the Shul."

"But it's late," Lech said.

"I know."

"I don't think it's wise to walk around at night," he said.

"We don't have a choice. Something worse might happen to your sister if we don't return to the Shul. I'm not a nurse or doctor. I don't know what to do in times like this."

I took a deep breath as I tried not to panic in the little boy's presence.

"Can you stay here alone tonight?" I asked him.

"Yes, but I won't be alone. I will be with your grandparents and Jasper," he said.

"That's good. Um...take the mat in my room and place it in my grandfather's room, okay? I don't want you to sleep alone. And lock all the doors. Are you sure you can do this?" I asked.

He nodded his head slowly. "I'll be fine."

We watched him as he walked back into the house. I wrapped my arms around Julia as I helped her walk down the road.

"I'm fine," Julia said.

"You're not fine."

"My brother is right, you know? It's not safe walking around at night. We could run into a German."

"Or you could die if we stay back at the house."

"We should have left a long time ago."

"How would you have coped like this?" I asked.

"I don't know. I don't know, Joanna. I'm scared, and that's all I know. I've lost my parents already, and I am not ready to lose my little brother, too."

We remained silent the rest of the way to the Shul, as we didn't want to draw attention to ourselves. It was a cold night and the moon was pale, bestowing a very dim light upon us. It was an uphill battle as I struggled to walk Julia to the Shul. Blood spurted from my injury and stained the white bandage wrapped around my leg.

"I can't walk anymore," Julia said. "I feel dizzy and want to lay on the bed."

"We're almost there," I said as I pointed to the Shul, which wasn't far away.

"Who is there?" someone said immediately.

"She needs help! She's a refugee," I said.

"What's wrong with her?" the man asked as we approached him.

The Shul was far busier than I had anticipated. Healthcare workers and refugees moved around quietly. The man put his arms around Julia, then led her to a table, where he told her to sit.

"You don't look so good yourself," a woman said. "Come, have a seat."

I squirmed on the uncomfortable wooden chair. My left leg felt numb.

"You're going to be fine," the woman continued.

"I don't think so."

"Why do you say that?" she asked.

"I don't know. Nowhere is safe anymore."

"Place your left leg on this stool. What's your name?" she asked.

"Joanna," I said as I followed her directions.

"That's a nice name."

"Thank you."

"How old are you?"

"I'm nine years old."

She smiled. "I had a daughter your age. Her name was Angelica."

"Where is she now?" I asked.

"She's dead."

My jaw almost dropped to the floor. I didn't realize she had used the past tense 'had' to talk about her daughter. And she had told me about the death of her daughter with a smile spreading across her face. I winced as she removed the blood-soaked bandage from my leg.

"She had long dark hair and one of the sweetest smiles ever," she said.

"I'm sorry for your loss," I said immediately.

"It's okay."

"Did she die in the war?" I asked.

"Oh no! She died four years ago. She was sick. Seeing you just reminded me of her. She would have been thirteen this November," she said.

I felt a bit relieved. "Okay."

"Is that your sister?" she asked.

I glanced at Julia. "No, she's a friend."

"How long have you been friends?" she asked.

"Not that long. She came here with her brother from Warsaw."

"I was a nurse in Warsaw, too. But here I am. I've never been here before. There's always a first time for everything."

"I'm going to leave here with my friends," I said.

"I'll stay here."

"Why?" I asked.

"People like you and your friend need me," she said.

"But it's not safe here. My friends and I will leave when we are strong enough."

"You said earlier that nowhere is safe, remember?" she asked.

"Yes."

"I'm going to give you something to stop the pain. I'll be right back," she said as she stood up from the chair. I glanced over my shoulders. Julia lay on the table as the nurse took care of her wounds. I heaved a sigh of relief, hoping that tomorrow would be a better day.

CHAPTER ELEVEN

The following afternoon, we were at the Shul when we heard the piercing cry of a man. This was followed by a gunshot in the far distance. For a few seconds, we were all quiet. Then we heard a second gunshot, followed by a series of continuous shots. The petrifying crackle roared around us, and the Shul broke into pandemonium. I shook Julia, who lay on the mat, unconscious.

"Julia! Julia!" I said. "Wake up! You need to wake up!"

She opened her eyes slowly. "What is it?" she asked.

"We need to leave."

She sat up, looking confused. "Oh my God! What's going on?"

"Everyone, get out! Get out! Run for your life!" people yelled from various corners of the Shul. Everyone scampered for their safety.

I placed my hands underneath her arm and tried to lift her from the mat. She groaned as she fell back to the floor.

"I can't stand it. I'm in pain," she cried out.

"If we don't leave now, we will die!" I said.

The Germans fired at us from everywhere. Blood spattered around us and people dropped dead like mangoes falling from a tree. There were shouts of "run," "save yourself," and "take cover."

I held her waist gently and wrapped her hands around my shoulder so that all her weight would rest on me. My left leg trembled tremendously as we staggered through the crowd of people scampering in pursuit of safety. Then, a fire broke out, and flames engulfed the Shul. We were trapped inside.

"You have to climb out of the building through the window," I said.

"I can't," she said.

"That's the only way!"

Julia grasped the lintel and placed her right leg on it. Then she screamed as she jumped out of it. I was about to jump through the window when someone pulled me back and jumped through the window in front of me. I got up immediately and jumped. I landed on the ground outside the

Shul. Sick people were trapped in the burning building and their cries reverberated in the air. There was no place to hide as bullets flew around us. Blood exploded out of a man's cheeks, and I screamed as the liquid splashed on my face. I crawled toward Julia, who lay on the ground.

"Let's pretend we're dead," I said as I lay on my back and closed my eyes. As the gunshots caused the air to vibrate, I prayed to God to spare our lives. The atmosphere had become contaminated with the smell of death, and I could feel the angel of death tugging at my hand, pulling me to a place of no return. My mind went to Babula and my grandfather. Lech was alone in the house with them, and I wondered if the killings had extended to places other than here.

Soon, someone stepped on Julia, and she cried out in pain.

"Get up!" I said. "Let's go!"

I pulled her up, and we staggered. I looked back and saw the Shul collapse while the fire raged and hungrily consumed the building. We escaped and left the Shul. Nothing much was left of Kaluszyn as we hurried back home.

———

I dashed to the burning building and tried to get into the house. Julia gripped my hand.

"You can't go in there!" she said.

"My grandparents are in there! Your brother is in there!" I cried out.

"You'll die!" she said.

I shook my head. "I can't stay back and watch them die."

"You don't know that. What if someone saved them already?" she asked.

"There's only one way to find out!" I said. The flames leaped and almost touched my body. I jumped back in fear. We stared at the angry fire that overtook the house. The heat burned my face. I tried to get into the house again, but the flames blocked the doors and windows.

"Help!" I yelled. "My grandparents are in there! Somebody, help!"

"Lech! Lech! Lech!" Julia cried out.

There was nobody to help us. Kaluszyn was like hell on earth that day. Every nook and cranny was on fire, and people were too busy saving themselves and what little assets they had.

"Babula! Grandpa!" I cried out as I ran around the house. "Lech! Lech! Can you hear me?"

"Lech!" Julia called out.

The air choked us as the burning buildings sent black smoke into the sky. We stared at the house in disbelief. Everything I had known for the past nine years of my life was being devoured right in front of me. Julia squatted on the ground, her head buried in her lap. I stood motionless.

"I was too late," I said. "I should have come earlier."

"It wasn't your fault, Joanna. You couldn't have known that this would happen."

Tears poured down my face. "Everything is my fault."

"It's the Germans' fault. They are the ones who want to take over everything," she said as she dug her hands into her hair. She groaned as she stood, and I hurried to help her.

"I'll be fine," she said. "I...I just...need to-"

I could tell she was holding back tears.

"I don't think Lech was in the house. He could have run off!" I said.

"He's just a small boy. He's the only one I have, and I don't know what I am supposed to do. What if he didn't make it? What if he couldn't leave?"

I opened my mouth to speak, but words failed to come out. Then we heard a bark! It was Jasper. He ran toward us, followed by Lech.

"Julia! Julia! Joanna! Joanna!" Lech yelled.

"Lech! Oh my goodness, it's you, Lech!" Julia said as she burst into tears. They hugged each other and cried. I wiped the tears off my face. I was glad he was alive, and I was eager to ask him about my grandparents. Jasper jumped on me as he moaned softly.

"I thought you were dead, Jasper! I'm glad you are alive!" I said.

After hugging his sister, Lech ran toward me and hugged me.

"We thought you were dead," I said. When I bent over to kiss his forehead, I saw that he looked tired, and his tousled brown hair smelled of smoke and dirt.

"I'm so sorry," he said as he burst into tears.

"Why are you crying?"

"It happened so fast," he said. His next words were choked with sobs, and I couldn't understand what he was saying.

"Calm down, Lech. Stop crying," I said.

"I couldn't...I couldn't save them!" he said. "I ran away from the house and couldn't get the...them...to walk. I'm sorry. I didn't mean to leave them behind. I...I...-"

"It's okay, Lech. It wasn't your fault. You did what you had to do," I said.

I could no longer hold in the heartbreak. I let go of him and fell to the ground. My grandparents were gone, and I was all alone. My lips trembled as I cried. Julia staggered toward me and wrapped her hands around me.

"We can't stay here," she said slowly. "We have to go."

"Go where?" I asked.

"Anywhere. We need to hide," she said.

"I don't want to hide. I don't want to leave. I want to stay here with my grandparents. I want to stay here with them."

She held my hands. "We're not safe here. We need to go into hiding."

I packed a handful of sand in my hand and threw it at the burning house. She tried to lift me, but I pushed her away.

"Let go of me," I said.

"Joanna."

"Let go of me!" I cried out. "I hate you Germans! I hate all of you! I hate every one of you!"

"Joanna!" Aleksander called from behind. He ran toward me and crouched in front of me.

"What happened?" he asked Julia.

Julia shook her head slowly. "The house-"

"Oh, no! Babula? Grandpa?" he asked.

"Yes," Julia said. "They didn't make it."

"Oh no!" he said as he burst into tears. "They burned our house, too."

"Really?" Julia asked.

"It's charcoal now! Nothing is left of it. Joanna?" he called me.

I didn't answer. I covered my face with my dirty hands.

"Joanna," he called again. He moved away from Jasper, who tried to grab his sleeve.

"Leave me alone," I said as I wiped the tears off my face. "I want to be alone."

"You can't be alone. We can't leave you here," he said.

"Leave me alone, Aleks. Go away!"

"You don't mean that," he said.

"I meant everything I said. Go away!"

"No."

"You don't understand!" I cried out. "You don't know how it feels to be all alone. I have no one else. My grandparents are dead! My baba is probably dead too, and my mama? I never got the chance to meet her! You can't understand how I feel right now. You-"

"Zofia and Jan are dead," Aleksander said.

I looked at him. "What?!"

"Yes. We couldn't save them. The Germans entered our house and shot them before burning the house down." His voice shook. "They found Jan and Zofia and shot them. They didn't see the rest of us as we hid in the house. My mama is badly hurt, and I don't know if she will survive. And we don't know where Hannah is. We haven't seen her since this morning."

"I'm so sorry, Aleks. I...I didn't know that. I can't believe this is happening to us. I don't want to die, Aleks. I don't want to die," I said.

"We're not going to die, I promise," he said.

"We have to leave now," Julia said. "We can't stay here anymore."

"Where do we go?" I asked.

"Follow the crowd. My dad said some people are running somewhere," Aleksander said.

"Where?" Julia asked.

"He doesn't know yet. We have to go and meet him now. He's waiting for us at the hill," he said. "Julia, can you walk?"

"I can manage."

"What about you, Lech?"

"I can walk," Lech said.

"Fine. Then we have to leave now," Aleksander said.

I stood and wiped my dusty knees and hands. I stared at the house for a long time. The fire had died, and I wanted to return to the house.

"There's no time," Aleksander said.

"I...I just want to see them for one last time," I said.

"There's still so much fire in there. What if the fire becomes bigger again and you are trapped inside?" Aleksander asked.

"Then it will be my fate to die with my grandparents," I said.

"No. I will come with you," he said.

"Are you crazy?" Julia said. "Listen to me, both of you. This is war! Lech and I have lost our parents in the war. That's what war does. It takes lives and renders people homeless. But there is still hope if we listen to Aleks and meet his father. That's what your grandparents would want, Joanna. They would want you to be safe. That was why they needed you to go with Mr. Vasilli, and they were willing to stay behind."

"She's right, Joanna. It's now or never," Aleksander said.

I stared at the house with a sense of loss that felt like a considerable part of myself had been taken from me. For years, I had heard about the various wars my father and grandfather had discussed. It was like a fairy tale. A myth that was never going to happen. My grandfather and father talked about the war because they had lived through the previous wars that had struck Poland. And now I was living mine. Only time would tell if I made it out alive to tell my side of the story.

CHAPTER TWELVE

Yarognev told us that we were going to a swampy field to seek shelter there because that was what most people were doing. If my grandfather and father were around, they would have mocked him.

"What does he know?" my grandfather would have said.

"This old fool!" my father would have said. "Now he thinks he can save us. Is he the messiah now?"

Yarognev was our messiah at that moment. We weaved through the woods to avoid German soldiers. We walked in a single file, with Yarognev behind everyone so that he could keep an eye on us. His friend led the way at the front of the line. A few other people also walked in the woods, hoping to get to the swampy field. It felt like the journey would never end.

Aleksander's mom could barely walk, and it seemed like she would crash to the ground. I could hear her heavy breathing behind me. I glanced over my shoulders occasionally because I feared she would drop dead soon. She plodded along, her eyes lifeless. She had two children left, and I could only imagine the pain she felt.

"Do you need anything?" Yarognev asked her.

"No," Milla said. Her response was almost inaudible. I could tell she was tired. She sounded like Babula when she was done cooking and had no strength to eat the food. I could tell that Milla had no strength to continue life.

As I walked, my leg sank to the ground. Jasper walked beside me. Lazor walked in front of me. He had not said a word since we came to join them on the hill. Even his eyes looked lifeless when he glanced back at me at some point in our journey. He was different from the chatterbox Lazor whom I was used to. Before the war, he would have bored me with long talks about things I didn't care about. And Jan would have yanked my hair if I wasn't paying attention. But today was different. The rest of our lives would be different, too.

Aleksander had told me that Lazor had watched the soldier shoot Jan. When everyone heard the gunshots, Jan and Zofia hid under the bed, while their mother hid under the bed in her room. Lazor hid behind a door, Aleksander hid inside a drum filled with water, and Yarognev hid in the bush at the back of the house. Lazor had hidden in a conspicuous place, yet none of the soldiers bothered to check the back of the door. Two soldiers barged into the house and searched everywhere. One of them entered the room and checked under the beds. They dragged Zofia and Jan out from under the bed, and Lazor could hear them screaming and begging for their lives. He could see them through the little crack in the door. Then he watched the man fire the gun without remorse, and Zofia and Jan dropped dead. Aleksander held his breath in the drum until the men dashed out and set fire to the house.

I wondered how Babula and my grandfather had suffered before they died. I wished I had been there to save them. I wish I had been there in their very last moments. My thoughts went to my father. Was he still alive? Or had he died at the cold hands of one of the soldiers? How many lives had he taken? I had never seen my father as one who would raise a gun to kill anyone. Was he cold and heartless like the German soldiers? Babula had told me that only cruel and brutal people committed crimes. They were the ones who stole, fought, and killed people.

"Nobody has the right to take the lives of others," Babula had said. "If you didn't create life, then you have no business taking it!"

"But people still kill other people. And they lie, cheat, and steal," I had said.

"That's because they are cold and heartless. If you have empathy, you will treat others with love and compassion. But if you are stone cold, you wouldn't bat an eye when you drove a sword into a person's chest."

Babula was right. Those German soldiers hadn't batted an eyelid when they fired their guns at us. Seeing dead people fall like fruit from trees was nothing to them. They stepped on us like we were mats and they killed five-year-old Jan. They killed children and babies, old and sick people, without batting an eyelid. They were more than men with cold hearts or monsters. They were demons that roamed the earth looking for people to take with them. I convinced myself that my father was different from the monsters that had assailed us. He was protecting us, and he was defending his home. The Germans were the ones who were greedy. They were the ones who wanted to conquer what wasn't theirs to begin with. So it wasn't wrong if my father had grown cold and heartless to kill off the Germans. At that moment, I wanted him to become like the German monsters. I wanted him to kill them all!

The woods were devoid of life. The air smelled of death and rotting vegetation. I noticed that the birds were missing from the trees, and even when the wind blew, the trees didn't move. It looked as if they were dead. Our future was marked with uncertainty. We weren't sure if we would survive the next minute, hour, or day. Any one of us could be dead at any time, and some might not make it to the swampy field Yarognev spoke about.

What would my life be like moving forward? I hadn't had time to think about it yet. I knew I wouldn't be around family, but at least I would be around Aleksander, Julia, and Lech.

Milla threw up behind me. We stopped walking and rushed to her.

"Mama!" Aleksander and Lazor cried out.

"Your injury has gotten worse," Yarognev said.

Blood spurted out of her stomach as she lay on the ground.

"Stop the bleeding," Yarognev's friend said. "Who has a piece of cloth around here?"

We looked at each other and shook our heads. Then, quickly, Yarognev tore the ends of his clothes and covered the bleeding wound.

"Her wounds are infected," his friend said. "We need a doctor."

"Where are we going to get one?" Aleksander asked.

Yarognev shook his head. "There's no way we can get one right now, and even if we get one, what about the medical supplies? We must try our best to take care of the wounds when we get out of here."

Milla looked pale, and her eyelids fluttered.

"Is she going to be okay?" Lazor asked Aleksander.

"Yes," Aleksander said immediately. "She will be fine."

"The blood is not stopping!" Yarognev said. His voice shook with fear. "I don't even know what I am doing anymore. The bullets are still in her belly. I don't know what to do!"

Lazor burst into tears. He thrust his face into Aleksander's belly and allowed his tears to soak his clothes. I couldn't stop my own tears from spilling from my eyes. Yarognev and his friend tried to stop the bleeding, but there was little they could do.

"Please don't die," Yarognev said to his wife. "Stay with us."

I wiped the tears off my face.

"Don't look," I said as I faced Aleksander. "It won't do you any good if you look."

"She's not going to die," Aleksander said.

"Take your brother away, Aleks. Just don't look."

He took Lazor, and they turned their backs away from us. Julia whispered in my ear, "She's going to die."

Milla's lips quivered as if she was trying to say something.

"What is it, Milla? Are you saying something? Don't worry; you will be fine," Yarognev said.

"Don't leave me," Milla said in hushed tones.

"I will never do that. I will be right here with you until you recover."

"Hannah…Jan," Milla said.

"I'm right here with you, Milla. You can do this," Yarognev said.

"I can see them," she said. "I can see my children. They need me."

Yarognev shook his head. "Lazor and Aleksander need you more here. Don't leave them behind. I need you to be strong for them."

I had been terrified when I saw a dead body for the first time at the Shul. I hadn't been able to sleep that night. Watching someone dying was much worse. A sudden chill crept up my spine. I pictured Milla preparing dinner back at their home and making some remarks about Yarognev. She knew he was usually within earshot, but she made those remarks anyway. And then Yarognev would say hurtful things, and the two would start bickering at each other. Aleksander and I would run off to the hill to avoid their daily squabble. But what I saw that day was two people who loved each other despite their differences. Yarognev held her hands and cried.

"Your hands are cold," he said. "Come back to me, Milla. I need you here. Your boys need you here."

I imagined holding onto Babula and Grandfather's hands. I wished I could hold my father's hands again, even if for just a second.

Yarognev glanced over his shoulders and looked at his children. The light had faded from his eyes. I saw raw pain hiding behind the false mask of bravery. He had two sons to protect, and he had to be brave for them. Though there was nothing else left to fight for, I knew he would fight for them. We locked gazes for some seconds before I broke off contact. I lowered my head and allowed the tears to flow down my cheeks. When I looked back at Milla, I knew she had left earth. Yarognev hugged her as tears racked his body.

We had no time to mourn the death of Milla. Gunshots reverberated in the woods, jarring loose all the birds that I thought had flown away. Quickly, we took cover.

"Run!" Yarognev yelled. "Save yourselves!"

The Germans had entered the woods and were shooting everyone. Adrenaline rushed through my veins. I started running, barely seeing what was in front of me. My feet flew over stones and leaves as I tried to get to the swampy field. The wind blew my hair back and smashed into my eyes. People entered the woods from the swampy field as we ran, and there was chaos.

"Go back!" they yelled. "Go back!"

As some of us ran to the fields, others were running back to town. I stopped running, then looked in the direction of the field and back to the town. I was confused, and I didn't know what to do. I couldn't find Yarognev, Lazor, Julia, or Lech.

"Jasper! Jasper!" I yelled out.

Time was passing quickly, and I needed to make up my mind. I hoped to find safety in the swampy field, so I continued running in that direction, my left leg feeling like it would explode. Instead, I ran out of the woods to find the chaos of people running helter-skelter. The Germans were everywhere, killing us.

"Joanna!" Someone called my name.

I glanced over my shoulder. It was Aleksander. And then I heard the gunshot, and blood exploded out of his belly. I ran toward him.

"Aleks! Aleks!" I cried out. "Please don't die. Don't die!"

I felt a firm grip on my arm. Someone lifted me and threw me over their shoulder.

"Let me go! Aleks! Aleks! Let me go! Put me down!" I begged.

He kept running, and I continued hitting his back as I called out Aleksander's name. I stretched my hands toward Aleksander, and Aleksander did the same. I wanted to hold him, caress his face, and tell him everything would be fine.

"Aleks!" My voice cracked as I screamed.

It happened so fast. A bullet pierced the man who carried me on his shoulders. The world began swirling, and I plunged to the ground. I felt dizzy, and my head pulsated. I felt my eyes close slowly. I wanted to stand, but I couldn't. I was paralyzed, slowly drifting away. Soon, all the thunderous noise filtered out, and all I had left was silence.

———————

I felt a sudden lash of cold air against my body. Birds chirped and whistled in the air. I wondered where I was. It felt like I had been picked up from the ground and thrown into the air. I thought I was flying. Then, in the sky, I saw Babula with colorful wings.

"You can fly, too?" I asked.

"Of course I can fly," she replied.

Babula looked different from what I was used to. She looked like the younger version of herself. She was more beautiful and agile.

"You can walk, too."

Babula chucked. "I can walk, too. So, you made it out of there. I'm so glad!"

"I wish I didn't," I said.

She touched my face. "Why would you think that way?"

"Everyone is gone. My family and friends are gone. What's the point of living when everyone else is dead?" I asked.

"There are so many reasons, my love."

"But you're dead! Grandpa is dead! My baba might be dead! Aleks is dead! Everyone is gone!"

"How would you have felt if your baba had lost hope when he lost your mama?" Babula asked.

"I don't know."

"Your father didn't lose hope, Joanna. On the contrary, he continued to have hope because of you. He entered the army because of you. He wanted to defend Poland because of you. Everything he did was because of you! If you had died, all his effort would have been wasted," she said.

"I'm lonely."

"No, you're not! You have us. Even if you cannot see us, we will always be right here with you," she said as she pointed to my chest.

She kissed my forehead. Then she disappeared and everything went dark.

"Babula!" I cried out. "Where are you?!"

I heard the slow whisper of my name floating in the air.

"Babula? Is that you?"

"Wake up, Joanna!" a voice said. "Wake up."

"Babula, is that you?"

"No, wake up."

I felt something cold on my toes. Slowly, I opened my eyes and saw a vague figure whose hair dangled over my face.

"She's awake," the voice said. "She has opened her eyes."

"Babula?" I asked.

"It's me, Julia."

I saw the smile that appeared on her face. Then, she held my hands and burst into tears. "Thank God you're awake. I was scared. I thought you were not going to wake up again."

Then something bit me and I jerked. It was Jasper.

"My God!" I gasped. "You're alive!"

Jasper barked as he licked my face. I burst into laughter and hugged him.

"I thought I had lost you!" I said as I looked around. "Where am I?"

"On a boat!"

I massaged my head with my hands as I looked around, confused. The last thing I remembered was seeing Aleksander falling behind me immediately after he was shot. Then, I remembered running back to him, holding him in my arms, crying. Next, someone grabbed me, pulling me away from him.

"Aleks? Where is Aleks?" I asked.

Julia kept silent. She looked away.

"Where's Aleks? Is he on the boat, too?" I asked.

She shook her head. "I don't know."

"What do you mean you don't know? Is he dead?" I asked.

"Joanna, I do not know if he is dead or alive."

"He was running on the field, and he got shot-"

"I saw him get shot, too. And then you ran to him."

"And someone grabbed me," I said.

"Yes, someone grabbed you," she said.

"Who grabbed me?" I asked.

"I don't know. He grabbed you and placed you over his shoulders as he ran to safety. Unfortunately, he got shot, and both of you fell. You must have hit your head on the ground because you passed out. Someone else carried you, and we ran to the ice factory at the edge of town. The owner let us hide in the cellar there. Nowhere else was safe, not even the swampy field."

"My goodness!"

"Mr. Vasilli was there."

"At the cellar?" I asked.

"Yes," she said. "Many people were there. They had been hiding for a while, waiting for a boat to carry them and some others out of Poland."

"I thought Mr. Vasilli and his family had left Poland after the first bombing," I said.

"It was just Mr. Vasilli who was in the cellar. His family couldn't make it."

"Is he on the boat now?" I asked as I looked around.

"Not this boat. He got on the other boat," she said. "I'm glad you are awake. Now I have company."

"Where is Lech?" I asked.

She looked away.

"Where is Lech?" I asked again.

"He didn't make it," she said in a trembling voice. "He couldn't get on the boat."

"I'm so sorry."

"It happened quickly. There were so many people trying to get on the boats. One minute I was holding him, and the next I wasn't. I searched around, but I couldn't find him. I thought he had gotten on the boat, so I got on. But he wasn't here either," she said.

"Maybe he is on the other boat," I said.

Julia exhaled deeply. "I hope so. I pray he is safe, wherever he is. Are you hungry?" she asked.

"Yes. Where did you get food?"

"That woman over there gave me bread. Not much is left, as I ate some of it, but it should keep you alive for a while," she said as she pointed to the woman.

The woman smiled at us when we looked at her. Julia handed the bread over to me, and I took it from her. I gobbled it, and then she gave me water to drink. The water wasn't much, but it was enough to push the bread down my belly.

"Who brought me on the boat?"

"That man over there. You should thank him when he wakes up because it wasn't easy carrying you on his shoulders amid all the shootings and bombings. And Jasper wouldn't let go of him. He followed him everywhere he went," she said as she pointed to the man.

I gasped as I saw Mr. Henryk.

"I know him," I said.

"From where?" Julia asked.

"He worked with my father. I can't believe he was the one who saved me."

"Me too. I didn't know you knew each other. I guess that explains a lot. Mr. Henryk was determined to save your life no matter what, and I'm glad he did," she said.

"Where are we going?" I asked.

"No one knows," she replied. "We were told Ukraine. I don't know, I'm not sure."

"The most important thing is that we get out of here," I said.

"Yes," Julia said.

Jasper lay on my lap and I stroked his dirty fur.

———

We didn't know where we were going, but we were glad we were far away from the war. I lay in a corner of the boat with Julia. I thanked Mr. Henryk when he woke up, and he was glad that I had regained consciousness.

"I knew you weren't dead," he said to me. "I'm glad you're alive!"

"I'm glad you're alive, too," I said.

"Jasper is a good dog. When he saw me with you, he followed us everywhere we went," he said.

We rarely spoke on the boat. Most of us preferred to be alone with our thoughts. The journey ahead of us was very far, and some of us might die before we reached a safe destination. However, I wasn't scared anymore. I had watched the people I loved die, and I was sure I wouldn't bat an eye if death came knocking at my door.

I lost count of the days we spent on the sea. We had no food and water, and we were all waiting on death. Jasper hardly barked and was always asleep. He had grown lean and I feared he would die, too. Some days, we had to throw a dead person overboard because there was nowhere to bury them.

"Why can't we leave them on the boat?" I asked Mr. Henryk.

"They will rot and smell."

"I just think it's cruel that we throw them over the boat," I said.

"If we left them here, those alive wouldn't be able to stay on the boat."

"The air will flush away the smell," I said.

"That's true. But the boat is too small, and the smell will linger."

After many days at sea, one day, Mr. Henryk's body was thrown overboard. Nobody noticed that he had been dead for a long time.

"He's been sleeping for hours," I said.

"He has been sleeping for hours since we got on the boat. I think that is how he copes with everything. He doesn't have to think while he is asleep," Joanna said.

"I think in my sleep," I said.

"What do you mean?" she asked.

"Anytime I close my eyes, I have nightmares. Then, when I'm awake, I daydream. I'm always thinking about what we've been through," I said.

That evening, Mr. Henryk still hadn't woken up. I crawled over and tapped him, but he didn't respond. I tapped him again. He didn't open his eyes or say anything.

"He's dead," someone said. And that was how he was thrown over the boat.

Finally, we got to Ukraine. It was a small town with people who were loving and welcoming. Our boat was crowded at the start of the journey, and I sometimes feared we would sink. However, there were only ten of us when we got to shore. The people fed and clothed us.

The woman who had given us bread on the boat wrote a letter to her cousin who lived in London. She would meet her cousin in a few days, and she asked us to accompany her.

"Yes," we said. "We will follow you to London."

Then I turned and ran. Jasper followed me, barking and wagging his tail. London wouldn't make me forget what I had been through, but I took it! With open arms, I took it and spent the rest of my days in Ukraine dreaming about the next phase of my life.

The End

Made in United States
North Haven, CT
04 December 2022

27850875R00095